OVERLORD

GALACTIC KINGS #1

ANNA HACKETT

Overlord

Published by Anna Hackett

Cover by Amalia Chitulescu Digital Art

Edits by Tanya Saari

ISBN (ebook): 978-1-922414-42-7

ISBN (paperback): 978-1-922414-43-4

WHAT READERS ARE SAYING ABOUT ANNA'S ACTION ROMANCE

Heart of Eon - Romantic Book of the Year (Ruby) winner 2020

Cyborg - PRISM Award Winner 2019

Edge of Eon and Mission: Her Protection - Romantic Book of the Year (Ruby) finalists 2019

Unfathomed and Unmapped - Romantic Book of the Year (Ruby) finalists 2018

Unexplored – Romantic Book of the Year (Ruby) Novella Winner 2017

Return to Dark Earth – One of Library Journal's Best E-Original Books for 2015 and two-time SFR Galaxy Awards winner

At Star's End – One of Library Journal's Best E-Original Romances for 2014

The Phoenix Adventures – SFR Galaxy Award Winner for Most Fun New Series and "Why Isn't This a Movie?" Series

Beneath a Trojan Moon – SFR Galaxy Award Winner and RWAus Ella Award Winner

Hell Squad – SFR Galaxy Award for best Post-Apocalypse for Readers who don't like Post-Apocalypse

"Like Indiana Jones meets Star Wars. A treasure hunt with a steamy romance." – SFF Dragon, review of *Among Galactic Ruins*

"Action, danger, aliens, romance – yup, it's another great book from Anna Hackett!" – Book Gannet Reviews, review of *Hell Squad: Marcus*

Sign up for my VIP mailing list and get your *free box set* containing three action-packed romances.

Visit here to get started: www.annahackett.com

CHAPTER ONE

She jogged up the front steps of the modern, glass building that housed the Nynatech offices. Seattle had kindly put on a sunny day with a gorgeous blue sky.

Mallory West didn't need to check her chunky Breitling Aviator watch to know that she was running late. She still had a few minutes to get to the pilots' locker room. She'd gone to bed way too late the night before. After yesterday's test flight, she and some of the other pilots had headed out to celebrate at their favorite little bar near Sea-Tac.

She'd only had one beer because she had a test flight today—a big one—but the others had gotten plastered and somehow managed to talk her into karaoke. She winced. It hadn't been pretty.

Mal pushed through the revolving glass door. She hadn't wanted to go out, but it had taken her mind off things and was better than sitting in her empty apartment.

Her gaze snagged on the coffee kiosk in the center of

the huge atrium lobby. Nynatech specialized in experimental space technology and were rolling in cash. They'd spared no expense for their head office. Glass walls and ceilings soared upward, and on the back wall, images played, showing all the company's products projected up in multi-colored glory. People in suits, or scientists in lab coats, bustled through, heading to the security turnstiles that led to the labs and offices.

Right now, all Mal needed was coffee.

There was only one person ahead of her in the line. She could nab a mocha with an extra shot and still make it upstairs before Dr. Francine Wheeler gave her hell for being late. The head of the Wormhole Drive project had a stick shoved up... Mal wrinkled her nose. The scientist was bossy, unfriendly, and didn't bother to hide her disdain for those she considered beneath her intellect. The woman had very little time for test pilots. She treated Mal and the others on the team without PhDs like a necessary evil.

Mal didn't give a shit. As long as she got her paycheck and got to fly, she was happy.

"Mallory!" Giovanni the jovial barista beamed at her. "Large mocha, extra shot, and extra chocolate?"

"Fix me up, Gio, my man." Mal swiped her card on the machine. "I am in *dire* need of caffeine, and I'm late."

"Oh, no." The older man started up the beast of a coffeemaker. "Dr. Wheeler won't be happy."

"Understatement, my friend. But nothing gets between me and my coffee."

"Big test flight today." Gio waggled his bushy eyebrows. "Are you nervous?"

Some small flutters took wing in her stomach. "More excited than anything. No time for nerves when you're rocketing through space."

Gio laughed, big and loud. "Not many of us get to do that. A bit different from the Air Force, yes?"

Mal pasted on a smile. "Right."

The flutters turned to knots in her gut. Her job now was way better than the rules and regulations of the Air Force. Mal loved to fly, and initially, she'd loved the Air Force. She'd been desperate to find her own place in the world.

But Mal was known for pushing the limits, especially as a combat pilot.

She'd disobeyed orders one too many times—for what she firmly believed were the right reasons. There'd been no way in hell she'd ever leave soldiers to die. She'd been dishonorably discharged for her trouble. Her gut soured. She wasn't sorry to have left, but it still left a bad taste in her mouth.

Luckily for her, Nynatech hadn't cared about her DD, and they liked that she pushed the boundaries.

"Here you go, Mallory." Gio handed her the biodegradable take-out cup—one of Nynatech's earlier inventions.

Mmm, the sweet, sweet scent hit her. The first sip was always the best.

Suddenly, she felt a sharp prick in her side.

"Don't scream or make a noise," a low voice said. "I want your security pass, now."

Gio froze, the ruddy color draining from his face.

Mal looked over her shoulder. The man behind her

was an inch shorter than her, a black ball cap pulled low over his face. She saw him swallow and noted the perspiration on his skin.

Her gaze dropped to the knife. "Dude, that is the sorriest excuse for a knife I've ever seen."

The man jolted. He had wide-set, brown eyes, and a lot of scruff. "Just give me your pass."

No doubt some guy with an axe to grind with Nynatech. Probably wanted to steal technical specs, or destroy something to stop the exploitation of space. It seemed like they had one or two crazies through here every month.

She saw the guy shoot some nervous glances toward the security guards by the turnstiles.

"Look, I can tell you've never used a knife for more than cutting your food," she said. "You're holding it wrong."

"What?" He shifted, clearly agitated.

"Yeah, my stepdad was a bit of an expert. Worked in the stunt industry and trained every day. Knives, swords, you name it. My mom died when I was eight, so Rusty raised me. He wasn't exactly sure what to do with a little girl, so he trained me to fight...with knives and swords, hand to hand." Mal smiled. "So, unluckily for you, you picked the wrong person to join you in this little knife fight."

The man blinked and swallowed again.

"And I was just about to have my first sip of a coffee I *really* need, and I'm running late."

"Look, lady—"

Mal shifted back and kicked the guy in the gut. He doubled over with an *oof*. With her free hand, she landed a punch to his face, then as he dropped the knife, she caught it before it hit the floor.

"See, this is how you hold it." She tossed the knife up, caught the hilt, and jabbed it in the air.

A solid front kick and the man flew into a display of chips and granola bars. Packets sailed everywhere, and the man fell to the tile floor in an ungainly sprawl.

She caught the gaze of the security guards and waved. Two sprinted over.

"You didn't even spill your coffee, Mallory," Gio breathed.

"Good, or I would have gotten really angry." She set the knife on the counter and sipped her coffee.

Yep, that first taste was always the best.

"I have to run," she said to the security guards. "You've got this?"

"Sure thing, West. Might need a statement later."

"Roger that. After I get back from Jupiter."

The guards grinned at her, hauling up her attacker between them.

Mal jogged to the turnstiles and swiped through. She decided the stairs would be quicker, and ran up to the pilot locker room.

Drinking her mocha as quickly as she could, she used her shoulder to barge into the locker room. Two pilots were sitting on the benches between the rows of blue lockers, chatting.

"West, you're late," one of the men said.

"Coffee emergency." She set her cup down and opened her locker. The first thing she did was take off her watch and carefully set it inside. Rusty had given it to her when she'd joined the Air Force. The military had cured her of any shyness, and she quickly shed her jeans and shirt. She pulled her high-tech flight suit out.

It was a deep, navy-blue with a touch of metallic silver at the seams. It fit her like a glove.

She wriggled into it. Gregson and Parker were both ex-military as well, and married. The sight of her black sports bra and panties was hardly going to drive them wild. She zipped the suit up to her neck.

"Wheeler was looking for you," Parker said.

"Great." Mal pulled her brown hair up in a tight ponytail.

She reached into her locker and pulled out a photo. The edges were crumpled. She was twelve in the shot, gangly, and still growing into her body. Rusty stood beside her. They were both holding swords.

He wore his favorite, battered cowboy hat. His skin was leather-brown and wrinkled from too much smoking and sun, and his hair was a mix of black and gray. He wore jeans and had a thick moustache that he'd never once shaved off. He'd been part cowboy, part stuntman, part wanderer.

Rusty had told her that he had too much tumbleweed in his blood to ever truly settle down. The longest he'd stayed in one place had been when her mother had been alive, but even then, he'd traveled for his work.

Mal ran a finger over the picture, pain piercing her heart. He'd died three months ago. He'd been larger than life, the only father she'd ever known. Sure, he'd had no idea what he was doing. He'd taken her to bars, taught her to fight, dragged her around the country to rodeos, movie shoots, and whatever jobs he picked up.

But she'd always known he was there for her. Sometimes, she barely remembered her mom. Just her soft voice and round face. When Mal looked in the mirror, she didn't see anything of her mom, except they had the same hazel eyes.

Rusty had survived so many injuries and bar fights, but years of smoking had finally done him in. He'd died of cancer. Of course, the crusty bastard hadn't told her he was sick until it was too late.

It doesn't matter how you die, Mal, it matters how you live. He'd said that to her just days before he'd died. She'd sat by his bedside, filled with a mix of terror, grief, and anger.

She stroked the photo again. He was gone and now she was alone.

Yes, she was about to turn thirty, but it still sucked to realize that if something went wrong with the test flight today and she never came home, no one would care.

"Mallory!"

Dr. Poppy Ellison strode toward her, her shoulder-length, blonde hair bobbing around her face. She was already in her flight suit, which hugged her petite body. Mal was five foot seven and toned muscle, Poppy was at least five inches shorter, and slender.

Well, one person would care if she didn't make it.

"Where have you been?" Poppy asked. "Dr. Wheeler is ranting."

"I'm right here. All ready to go."

Poppy was the head scientist for the wormhole drive.

She was super-smart, straightforward, and in possession of a killer eyeroll for fools. She treated Mal to one now.

Mal grinned. When she'd first come to work at Nynatech five months ago, she'd never guessed that she'd actually like any of the scientists, let alone become best friends with one.

Somehow, despite their differences, she and Poppy got on like they'd known each other for years.

A door banged open, and the tall, painfully thin form of Dr. Francine Wheeler strode in.

Ugh.

"West, you're late," the scientist said.

"I'm ready when you are, Doc."

Wheeler shot her a hard stare. "Both of you out to the launch pad. Need I remind you that this is an *extremely* important test for Nynatech? History-making."

Yeah, yeah. You're a special snowflake and I'm a lowly pilot.

"We're ready, Dr. Wheeler." Behind the doctor's back, Poppy made a face and jerked her head at Mal. *Don't talk back. Let's just get going.*

Mal sniffed. *I'm just standing here.*

Poppy grabbed Mal's arm and hauled her out of the locker room. "Let's go to space."

Mal wiggled her shoulders, shaking off her tension. "Let's do it."

"CONTROL, all systems are green, and we're in a stable orbit," Mal murmured into her headset. "The view is *spectacular*."

She finessed the controls of the sleek, experimental starship. Outside, the Earth was a beautiful, blue-green orb suspended in the black of space.

She smiled and shifted in the curved seat that molded to her body. Sensors in the chair were monitoring her vitals. It didn't get much better than this: getting paid to test experimental starship technology with the best view in the solar system.

"Acknowledged, Hotshot One. Stay in position while we finish diagnostics."

Mal raised a brow at the control panel. "Hotshot One? That's the best you could come up with, Simmons?"

Her controller, back on Earth in the control room in the Nynatech office, snorted. "It suits you, West."

"I'm not buying you an after-test beer. Hotshot? That's so lame."

"Well, you can be a bit hotheaded sometimes."

"I'll show you hotheaded," Mal drawled.

"Keep the comm line clear," the sharp voice of Dr. Wheeler cut across the line.

She was probably looming over Simmons' shoulder. Mal pulled a face.

"Let Dr. Ellison finish her calibrations in peace," Dr. Wheeler added.

Mal switched to the internal comm line. "How you doing back there, Poppy?"

Poppy was seated behind Mal in the tight cockpit of the experimental ship.

"What?" Poppy sounded a little preoccupied.

"How's it going?" Mal repeated.

"Everything's fine. I just need to finish calibrating the wormhole drive conductor."

"Take your time." Mal didn't want to get Poppy started on all the science speak. Mal's eyes usually glazed over, and her brain went numb.

She grabbed a jar of peanuts from the pocket of her seat. She popped some in her mouth. She'd gotten addicted to the things in the Air Force. From the hours of sitting on a tarmac, waiting to be called up for an extraction. She hummed a little under her breath, checking her systems. All good.

She had a few days off coming up. She tapped her short nails on the console. Maybe she'd head to the beach somewhere. Warm sand, cold beers, a hot one-night stand with a surfer, and some snorkeling.

Normally, she'd spend her time off with Rusty.

Her stomach contracted. *God.* She rubbed her chest. It was still hard to believe he was gone. He'd left her his old truck, and his sword and knife collection.

Stay focused, Mal. "Poppy? How's it going?"

"Mal, this isn't like tuning a car engine."

"Hell, Pop, I don't even know how to tune a car engine."

"Sorry." Poppy blew out a breath that echoed over the line. "This isn't easy and it isn't like there's an instruction manual when you're doing something for the first time."

"Well, Rusty used to say that if the road is easy,

you're likely going the wrong way."

"Sounds like your stepdad had a saying for everything."

Mal smiled. "He sure did."

"Well, I'm almost there. I definitely want to get this right."

Hell, yeah, she did. They were testing an experimental wormhole drive technology. They definitely needed it right.

Especially when it was based on alien technology.

Over a year ago, the Fortuna Science Space Station orbiting Jupiter had been attacked by an alien ship.

It'd been a hell of a shocker of a first contact. Mal remembered watching the news and reports in horror. The space station had been ruined, and most of the scientists and station staff killed. A lucky few—or unlucky, depending how you looked at it—were abducted by alien slavers. The aliens had used a transient wormhole to travel to Earth's solar system, and they'd used it to leave again. Back to the other side of the galaxy.

As Earth had set about salvaging the destroyed space station, those who were taken were assumed lost.

Until they'd made contact with Earth using micro-wormhole technology to send messages back.

The survivors had contacted their loved ones. They'd been taken in, and were now living on the other side of the galaxy on a desert planet called Carthago.

Mal shook her head. Those poor people. They had no way home, and were now making a life on an alien planet. The good news was that they also sent advanced technology specs back to Earth.

Nynatech had won the bid to develop the new wormhole drive. The goal was a new, faster method of space travel.

The big test was today, and it should create a wormhole large enough for their ship. The plan was for her and Poppy to travel through it to Jupiter in the blink of an eye.

She was looking forward to seeing the new space station being built. The Resilience Station was currently under construction.

"Okay, Mal," Poppy said. "I think we're ready."

"Think?"

The scientist took a deep breath. "No, it's ready."

"You okay, Poppy?"

"Yes. Just excited. We're making history here, Mal."

"We sure are. Ready to see Jupiter?"

"Absolutely," Poppy replied.

Mal touched the comm. "Control, we're ready to conduct the test."

"Acknowledged, Hotshot One," Simmons said.

She rolled her eyes.

"Hotshot One?" Poppy said. "That's the best he could do?"

"Simmons isn't known for his sparkling wit."

"I can hear you," Simmons said dryly.

"I know," Mal said.

Simmons ran her through the pre-test checklist. Mal checked everything three times. She might like to take a few risks sometimes, but not with technology that was about to fling her seven hundred million kilometers through space.

"Control, we're ready when you are." She switched to

the internal comm. "Poppy, you strapped in?"

"I'm ready."

But Mal heard the woman's nerves in her voice. Mal released her own breath. "Initiating flight test."

The ship's regular engines fired, and the ship shot forward.

Mal loved this little baby—she was a sleek, sexy beauty.

"Countdown to wormhole drive initiation." *Here we go.* "Three. Two. One." Mal touched the controls.

The ship launched forward at blinding speed. Sparks of blue light washed over the front of the fuselage, then everything around them turned to a streaming, blue glow. She was thrown back in her seat.

"It's working!" Poppy cried.

"Data is coming through, Hotshot One," Simmons said. "We need...get...by—"

"You're breaking up, Control," Mal said.

Suddenly, the ship was tossed sideways.

What the fuck? Mal was thrown hard to the side, her harness digging into her shoulder.

Poppy screamed.

They started spinning over and over. Pops of blinding light speared into Mal's eyes. Gritting her teeth together, she pushed forward. All the controls were flickering.

No, dammit. "Control, abort. Abort!"

She shoved her hand on the emergency stop. There was a violent jerk, and the ship spun again.

The blue glow stopped, but the ship was still flying out of control. Everything was vibrating.

"Mal!"

"Hold on, Poppy." She gritted her teeth so hard she tasted blood. She fought for some control. Nothing was responding.

Mal looked up and gasped. There was a huge planet ahead—dark blue and green. Beyond it was a giant red star.

It wasn't Jupiter.

It wasn't any planet she knew.

The ship was caught by the planet's gravitational pull. Alarms blared.

"Poppy, we're going to crash land. Hold on and brace!"

"Mal, the star maps... They don't match anything. Where are we?"

Only Poppy would be checking star maps in the middle of crashing.

"Brace!" Mal yelled.

They hit the atmosphere. The ship shook. Mal ground her teeth, and finally got some response out of the controls. She tried desperately to slow them down.

The next thing she knew, a rocky landscape spread out below them, dotted with sharp rock formations.

Hell. They were coming down too fast.

"Poppy!"

Boom.

There was a huge explosion. For a second, Mal was aware of things breaking, crunching, and tearing apart.

Everything was spinning. She heard screaming and realized it was her own.

Something hit her head, and then there was only merciful darkness.

CHAPTER TWO

He slashed one of his swords down in a wide arc, catching the alien creature in the shoulder. It reared up on its back legs and snarled.

The hexid was a huge creature that walked upright on its two muscular back legs, but often ran on all fours. Its body was hairless, covered in taut, almost transparent skin that revealed its organs underneath. Its wide shoulders were hunched, its powerful, overlong arms ended in three sharp claws, and its jaw held fangs designed to rip and tear.

The smell of rot, decay, and its fetid breath hit him. It was an abomination. And he didn't want it on his planet.

Overlord Rhain Zhalto Sarkany swung both his swords. The bleeding hexid dodged, its powerful body flexing.

No. Rhain slashed. First sword, then his second. The hexid fell.

All around him, his elite fighters battled more hexids.

They swung swords and axes; some were armed with crossbows.

He would not lose more people.

Not to this evil sent by his father.

He saw a large hexid leap up and take down one of his fighters.

No.

Rhain whirled. He pulled on the power he felt all around him from the magnetic field of the planet. His species had evolved to utilize it.

Power filled his veins, his cells. It thrummed through him, his skin glowing with a faint, red sheen. It charged his two swords and red lights lit up along the specially crafted blades.

With a growl, he leaped high, the energy lifting him into the air.

He reached the hexid and brought his glowing blades down.

The creature released its prey and snarled, but Rhain's dual swords bit deep.

The hexid snapped its fangs. Rhain dodged and sliced his blade along the creature's leather-like skin.

Innards spilled out, putrid and black. He saw several bits of metallic tech amongst the organic matter. The work of the Zhylaw: a species known to use biotechnology for terrible purposes.

He fought back a sneer.

He cut again and the hexid collapsed.

Chest heaving, he turned to his injured fighter. The young man had a hand pressed to the two deep gashes on his abdomen.

Rhain helped him up. "Let's get you to the medicas."

"Yes, Overlord. Thank you."

Rhain stayed close to the limping man as they crossed the battlefield. His fighters had almost finished with the pack of hexids. This area consisted of lush, green fields. There were farmlands to the west, and to the east, the rocky, wild land of the Barrens. The hexids had slipped out of the Barrens and attacked a mining transport. Rhain and his fighters had been close enough to hear the screams.

The medica ground transport stood to the side. The large rugger was beige in color, and drove on six huge wheels, perfect for all types of terrain.

Two medicas, their metallic armor touched with green, hurried out. They whisked the injured fighter inside.

Swords still in hand, Rhain turned to scan the battlefield. Most of the hexids were down. He saw one of his fighters use a charged axe that glowed orange to cut the head off a snarling animal. His men and women moved with well-trained precision. Zhaltons had always been fighters. To survive the Radiance and its effects, they'd had to be.

His jaw tightened. The hexids weren't native to Zhalto. They were an abhorrence sent here to destroy.

The Zhylaw used technology to push beyond what was right and wrong. The hexids were genetically modified, and kept alive past their natural lifespans, which helped turn them wild and crazed. They became violent killers.

Suddenly, a hexid bounded out from behind a transport. With a powerful leap, it landed on the roof of the rugger, setting it rocking.

It crouched, its soulless, black eyes fixed on Rhain.

It leaped.

He whipped his swords up, but he was well aware that the hexid would hit him first.

A powerful body leaped in from the side, wielding a single straight sword. It was fully charged and glowing gold.

Rhain watched his captain of the guard, Captain Thadd Naveri, slice into the alien animal.

The hexid roared, but Thadd's charged blade moved blindingly fast.

The creature fell. Thadd pulled his bloody sword free and straightened.

Rhain's best friend and right-hand man's metallic armor was splattered with gore, just like Rhain's.

"You stole my kill," Rhain said.

Thadd snorted. "It was about to disembowel you."

Thadd was a little taller than Rhain, and much broader. When he wasn't by Rhain's side, he was training, and every inch of him was solid muscle. He kept his brown hair cut short, and his eyes were a brilliant blue.

They stood shoulder to shoulder.

"This is the third hexid attack this week." Thadd's voice vibrated with rage.

Rhain slid his swords away in the scabbards on his back. His fingers flexed.

"Yes," he said darkly.

His gaze flicked up. A huge moon hung overhead, but

beyond it lay the distant outline of three planets. The larger one in the distance was Sarkan.

His father's planet.

Rhain's nostrils flared.

His *gorr* of a father had allied with the Zhylaw. The Zhylaw were supplying King Zavir Sarkany with an army of creatures like the hexids.

A month ago, Rhain's father had started a brutal campaign on Rhain's planet. He wanted Rhain to join him and stand at his side.

Rhain had not-so-politely refused.

But a man like Zavir—ruthless, cold, and hungry for power—never took no for an answer.

Rhain would fight to the bitter, bloody end to protect his people from his father. Because it was his duty, and in memory of his beloved mother.

"Load up the wounded. Burn the hexid bodies." A nice gesture to his father, plus it destroyed the tech the Zhylaw used so it couldn't be recycled.

More rugger ground transports rumbled in on large wheels.

The medicas and unwounded fighters loaded the injured on board the transports.

Rhain needed to contact his brothers. They needed to be updated and warned. Their father would be coming for them next.

The Sarkany system had five planets orbiting a red-giant star. Sarkan was his father's planet, and most distant from the sun. The Sarkans had always been violent, warlike, disturbing the peace in the system. His father ran the planet with a brutal, unforgiving rule. He controlled everything his people did, suppressed all dissent, and his army trained rigorously.

Ask any Sarkan about their king and they'd paste on a smile and extol all the virtues of their wonderous leader.

Zavir wasn't content with ruling his planet. No, he wanted to control the entire system.

Three other planets— Zhalto, Damar, and Taln— were home to related species, and they'd all adapted to their own planet's environments. The fifth planet, closest to the sun, was an uninhabitable rock called Andret. It was mineral rich, but home to vicious native creatures that made any exploration difficult.

Years ago, Zavir had come to power and decided to conquer the system. After intense fighting with the people of Zhalto, Damar, and Taln, all four planets had been pushed to the brink. Then Zavir had proposed peace.

Through marriage.

Or rather, marriages.

He'd taken a bride from each planet in return for peace.

Rhain tried not to tense up. His mother had gone to her marriage resolute. She'd hated Zavir, but she'd loved her planet. And she'd loved Rhain.

But Zavir hadn't wanted peace. He'd wanted to breed sons with unique abilities of each of the species.

Millennia ago, the Sarkany System had been less advanced, with five lush, habitable planets orbiting the sun.

Until the Radiance.

A massive, powerful solar flare had ripped through the system.

It had torn away the atmosphere of Andret, and destroyed the people living there. It had gone on to irradiate the other planets.

On Zhalto, the Radiance had cut through a part of the planet, leaving behind the rocky Barrens. It had also interacted with the planet's magnetic field, making it stronger, and leaving it laden with a flow of charged particles emanating from the sun. Their species had adapted and learned to manipulate the charged particles in the field and use the powerful energy.

On Damar, the Damari people had changed. Many died, but the survivors became stronger, wilder. It left them with the ability to shapeshift form into wild, wolf-like animals.

The Taln had darker, powerful abilities linked to their planet's geology. They could command the very dirt and rocks of their planet.

Sarkan was just far enough away to not suffer any ill-effects from the Radiance. They had no special abilities, and compensated with their ruthless violence.

Rhain had a half-brother from both Damar and Taln. None of them cared about the half, and they all shared a hatred of their father.

But Zavir wanted his sons at his side, and he always had. And now, he was using his alliance with the Zhylaw to force the issue.

"Not today, Father," Rhain murmured. "Not ever."

Suddenly, a boom cracked through the evening sky.

Rhain jerked his head up and stiffened.

Flames cut across the sky, falling fast.

Thadd made a sound. "That looks like debris."

"Starship debris," Rhain said.

One large piece disappeared from view. Near the Badus Mountains in the heart of the Barrens.

The second large piece sailed right over their heads.

The crash was close enough to shake the ground.

"Thadd, tell Cayna to get the injured back to Citadel. Then handpick your best fighters. Let's go and investigate."

Thadd frowned. "This could be a trap of your father's."

"Highly likely." Rhain's lips turned into a grim smile. "If it is, I'll make him regret it."

MAL OPENED her eyes and groaned.

Everything hurt, like she'd been through a meat grinder. She was still in her seat, but tipped over. With another groan, she managed to hit the release on her harness.

Ow, ow, ow.

She shifted and fell on her hands and knees. Twisted metal lay all around her.

Fuck.

It didn't even look like her ship anymore.

She ripped her headset off. "Poppy? Poppy?"

There was no response.

Steeling herself, and willing her muscles to move, Mal pushed up and turned.

Dizziness swamped her and she almost went down. She locked her knees. Then her stomach simply dropped away.

The back of her ship... Was gone.

"No!" She shuffled forward. "No, no, *no*."

Poppy's seat was gone. Only half the console was still visible.

Mal's chest tightened. She tried to pull in air. "No...Poppy."

Goddammit to hell. Mal tried to think, but all she wanted to do was scream. The test had gone wrong. Hell, that was the understatement of the century.

She scanned the green field around her. It was covered in a carpet of pretty, blue flowers shaped like bells. In the distance, she could see a clump of strange rock formations. They looked like something out of an apocalyptic movie. She noticed that the sky seemed a little darker blue, and she eyed the setting sun.

It had a distinct red tinge to it.

Turning slowly, she saw the huge outline of the moon hanging in the sky. And the faded outlines of several celestial bodies.

Wherever she was, it wasn't Earth.

Her heart knocked hard against her ribs. So where the hell was she? Was there a chance Poppy had made it?

She walked down the length of the wreckage, biting her lip to stop crying out from the aches and pains shooting through her. There might be something she could salvage. Thankfully, her spacesuit was still intact.

She felt a sharp pain in her gut and looked down. A small bit of steel was protruding from her stomach.

Okay, mostly intact.

She gripped the shard and pulled it free.

"Oh, shit." She clamped her hand over the wound and groaned. "Don't pass out. Don't pass out."

She waited for her head to stop swimming. A nasty headache throbbed, and she pressed a hand to her temple and hissed. Her skin felt itchy, and when she swallowed, there was a nasty metallic taste in her mouth.

She couldn't spot much in the smoking wreckage.

A sense of desolate aloneness washed over her. *What now? Where did she go?*

She clenched her hands together and looked at her boots. She dragged in a deep breath. It was Rusty's smoky voice she heard in her head. *You can find a way, or bury your head in the sand, girl. Both require digging.*

"Okay, time to think, Mal." The sun was setting, so it would be dark soon. She needed shelter. She decided to head for the rocks.

A low growl made the hair on the back of her neck stand on end.

She turned slowly and sucked in a deep breath.

A huge, fucking *thing* was slinking toward her.

It had to be nearly seven feet tall. It had huge, muscular back legs, and long arms tipped with claws. Big claws. It hunched a little, and its skin was leathery, desiccated. It was white-gray and she could see...*ew*, its organs beating and pumping.

It snarled, showing her big teeth, and inky-black eyes that looked creepy.

Slowly, Mal crouched and pulled a long piece of metal out of the wreckage.

She'd kill for her favorite Scorpion tactical katana. *Crap.* Her beloved weapons collection was far, far away.

She rose and hefted the metal.

The creature moved closer.

"Nice, monster thing." She lifted her makeshift weapon higher. "Look, ugly thing with lots of teeth, I just survived a starship crash. I'm really not interested in getting mauled or eaten. I mean, I deserve a break."

It growled again.

"Yeah, well, of course you'd disagree. I don't suppose you're slow-moving?"

It leaped up onto the smoking ruin of her ship—lithe, powerful, agile.

And fast.

Yeah, no break for Mal. Story of her fucking life.

The creature rushed her.

She braced and swung the metal like a bat.

It connected with the creature's huge skull, and it let out a deep grunt, then swung around, jaws snapping.

Mal dived and rolled across the ground, crying out at the host of aches and pains. Thankfully, a surge of adrenaline helped her leap to her feet.

The animal watched her, baring its teeth.

Oh, what big fangs you have.

She tightened her grip on the metal. The creature leaped and she threw herself sideways. The animal darted past Mal, and she ran, leaping on top of her ship wreckage.

She spun.

The beast turned, watching her like it was trying to formulate a plan of attack.

Mal braced. "Come on!"

It leaped.

Really high.

Oh, fuck.

It sailed right at her. She swung the metal, but couldn't stop the beast's momentum. It rammed into her, knocking her off the ship, and she flew backward.

Mal hit the ground flat on her back with an *oof*. The air rushed out of her.

Move, Mal. Move.

She rolled.

Huge fangs snapped together right near her face.

Hot, rotten breath, and the sickly scent of decay, washed over her. Her gaze landed on some circular metal embedded in the skin of the animal's thick neck.

What the hell was that?

She rammed her piece of metal up and jammed it against the implant.

The beast roared.

Mal rolled again and climbed to her feet. An intense wave of dizziness hit.

No. She gritted her teeth. If she collapsed now, she was going to get eaten.

The beast circled her. She saw a glimpse of that metal implant again. She'd dented it. She lifted her weapon. Then, she raced at the beast and landed a solid whack to its side.

It whipped around, and she followed, giving it another heavy hit. It yelped.

Mal smiled. "Don't like that?"

Surprising her, it lunged to the side, bumping into her. She staggered, almost losing her balance.

The creature leaped at her, long arm swinging. She felt the sharp slash of claws against her suit as it cut across her stomach.

The wet slide of blood oozed across her belly.

Another hit of rancid odor seared her nostrils. She dropped down and rolled under the creature's legs.

Then she rammed her metal up into its gut.

It howled. Warm, black blood splattered over Mal.

She turned her head, then jerked the metal hard, cutting a jagged slash down the beast's belly. It took two wobbly steps and collapsed. Mal managed to just roll out of the way.

Phew. She stayed where she was, lying flat on her back, and stared up at the stars appearing in the night sky. She saw a nebula—bright and pretty.

Definitely not on Earth.

With a sigh, she staggered to her feet.

Ow, she really, really hurt now. Her skin was tingling, and her headache was approaching monstrous proportions.

On the ground, the beast moved weakly.

No, you don't. She lifted her piece of metal and smashed down on the creature's head. Then again. And again. Damn, it had a thick skull.

Chest heaving, dizzy, she heard a roaring sound in her ears.

No, wait. That was the sound of an *engine.*

She turned and almost lost her balance again.

A rugged vehicle, unlike anything she'd seen before,

rumbled into view. It looked like an ATV on steroids. It was tan colored with six huge wheels, and an engine that glowed bright blue at the back.

She lowered the chunk of metal and used it to lean on.

Doors on the side of the vehicle rose open, and several people climbed out.

Big, muscular people.

Oh, shit. They wore high-tech-looking suits in dark metallic gray, touched with some red. They all had "badass fighter" written all over them. There were five men and one woman. Each one was holding a weapon.

They stared at her, her ship, and then the dead beast.

A man strode forward.

A hell of a man.

Mal straightened. He wore a molded, metallic armor over his powerful chest with a medallion set in the center, and it showed every carved muscle in his torso and abdomen. Her gaze snagged on the corded muscles of his biceps, and he had thick bracer-like bands on his fore-arms. High-tech leather pants tucked into heavy boots and the hilts of two swords peeked over his broad shoulders.

He managed to look like some futuristic barbarian warrior come to life.

His steps were sure, unhurried, like a predator who knew he was the top of the food chain. He looked like he owned the place. Power throbbed off him, and she could feel it on her skin, like she'd gotten too close to a fire.

Liquid-silver eyes met hers. She felt the weight of that gaze, loaded with power and authority. The breeze made his longish, black hair dance around his face. *That face.* Mal felt every feminine instinct inside her sit up and do the rhumba. Strong jaw, rugged lines, aggressively masculine.

He said something in an unfamiliar language and gestured at the dead beast. His voice was deep, with a touch of sexy grit. It also had that confident, decisive ring to it that only people used to giving orders could pull off.

She rubbed her cheek. Oh crap, she was covered in blood.

"I have no idea what you're saying—" she pointed at the beast "—but I killed that, yes."

The man's eyes churned like molten metal. He started talking again.

"Hey, big guy in charge, sorry to interrupt, but I'm going to pass out now."

All of Mal's strength left her. Her headache clamped on her skull with a claw-like grip, making her want to whimper.

As she pitched forward, the last thing she saw was the warrior lunging to catch her.

CHAPTER THREE

Rhain lifted the woman into his arms.

She didn't weigh as much as he'd expected. He didn't recognize the design or color of her spacesuit.

His gaze traced over the strong lines of her face. She had a small scar that bisected her left eyebrow and a small, dark mark high on her right cheekbone. Before she'd passed out, he noted that she had unique eyes—a pale green, with gold flecks.

"Looks like remnants of a ship." Thadd eyed the smoking wreckage.

"Scan it," Rhain ordered. "She needs a medica."

His captain lifted his wrist and touched his projecta band. Blue light projected up and Thadd swiped through it, then a beam of light shot out and scanned the smoldering ruins of twisted metal.

Narla, one of his fighters, stepped forward. She crouched by the dead hexid. "That female took down a hexid... With a hunk of metal."

Yes, she had. Rhain shifted the unconscious woman's

weight. "I'll get her aboard the rugger. Make it quick, Thadd, I want to get back to Citadel."

The side of the rugger was open, and a fighter with a charged sword stood to attention, standing guard.

Rhain strode straight up the ramp and settled on one of the seats that lined both sides of the vehicle.

The woman stirred. He saw that she'd been clawed by the hexid and was bleeding. She bled red like them, but her musculature was not as dense as a Zhalton.

She wasn't from here.

He fingered her brown hair. It felt like gossamer silk. Much finer than Zhalton hair.

Finally, his fighters boarded.

Rhain nodded at the driver. He felt a familiar flare of energy as the rugger's engine powered up.

They set off across the green landscape.

"The scan?" Rhain asked.

"The ship was a mix of metals of some sort," Thadd said. "Not particularly strong. No signs of nadian or craxma."

The most common metals used in any vehicles or ships in the Sarkany system.

"So, she's not from here." That didn't rule out her being one of his father's agents. Zavir was smart and cunning.

"Her technology appears...primitive," Thadd said.

"We'll know more once she wakes." Rhain looked down at her. It appeared that her nose had been broken once before and hadn't healed correctly.

One thing was for sure, she was a warrior.

She'd survived a crash, and taken down a hexid alone.

That meant she was tough.

And dangerous.

Yes, Zavir knew Rhain well enough. Knew Rhain would render aid to someone in trouble, especially a woman. His father was clever enough to send a spy in who would slip under Rhain's defenses.

He couldn't allow that to happen.

He glanced out the rugger's windshield. The last rays of the sun were almost gone. They were close to the Barrens here, and sometimes beasts slipped out to hunt. But in his head, he was remembering Renkitis Outpost. It had been a farming community, attacked by his father's creatures a few days ago. They'd slaughtered everyone.

Rhain's hands tightened on the woman, darkness stirring in his chest. No one killed his people and got away with it. If this woman was one of his father's agents, she would die.

The vehicle jolted over some rough ground, but soon, they reached a main road to Citadel, and picked up speed.

He held the female fighter tighter. She made a small sound, her face pressed against the fabric of his armor. She had skin touched with gold, and very long eyelashes.

"Careful, Rhain," Thadd said. "We have no idea who she is, or where she comes from. No idea how dangerous she is. It is very likely your father sent her. She could be Zhylaw."

"She's not Zhylaw." The Zhylaw were smaller, more compact, with dark hair and dark eyes. They'd long ago stopped using their bodies for physical means, and depended more on their brains.

They weren't warriors.

Finally, the farmlands and fields of rainbow-colored flowers gave way to the forests near Citadel. They'd be home soon.

Night had fallen, and auroras filled the sky in greens, blues, and pinks—dancing and dipping. Every night, thanks to the planet's strong magnetic field, they were witnesses to the extraordinary lights in the sky.

The mountains and Citadel appeared.

The mountains formed a roughly circular valley, and the city of Citadel was nestled inside. The rugger drove up the large, stone bridge leading to the fortified entrance to the city.

The gates opened and they drove through.

Every time he saw his city, Rhain's chest filled with warmth. Buildings of gleaming white stone cascaded down the sides of the mountains, and large terraces cut into the cliffs bustled with life. Towers speared into the air, topped with roofs of red and gold metal. Trees grew in pots and garden beds dotted all over the city.

They drove over a bridge, crossing over the lake in the center and headed for the royal palace.

This was where Rhain had grown up, knowing he would one day rule. His mother had refused to let him go to Zavir and Rhain had been happy to stay here. This was his home.

Several palace guards stood to attention at the palace's main entrance, waiting for them.

An older man stood to the side, a floating stretcher beside him. The medica had dark skin, gray hair cut short, and pale-blue eyes. He was old, an extremely talented healer, and generally straight forward to the point of rudeness. Not that Tavith cared. He only cared about healing his patients.

Rhain climbed out of the rugger, carrying the still unconscious woman in his arms. He was strangely reluctant to let her go. There was something about her...

He wasn't sure what. He couldn't sense any energy off her. Like most visitors to Zhalto, she wasn't adapted to their planet, unable to use its energy field.

"Auroras above." The medica's eyes widened, taking in the woman. "What have you brought me, Overlord?"

"We found her in the ruins of her crashed ship."

"Bring her." Tavith waved at the stretcher.

Rhain set her down.

The medica frowned. "She isn't Zhalton."

"No. Can you tell her species?"

The medica touched his projecta band and his screen projected up in the air. He studied the data and then shook his head. He held a palm over her face, just off her skin.

Rhain felt a flare of energy and saw a faint green glow on the man's hand. The medica pulled energy to him, manipulating it to assess and heal.

Rhain could manipulate it to kill.

All Zhaltons could access the energy field, to varying degrees. Some barely felt it at all, while others from the powerful houses bred and trained their children to strengthen their abilities.

The Zhalton royal family were the strongest wielders of all.

"I don't know what she is, but she needs to be in my medica ward."

Rhain waved to Thadd to handle the fighters, and followed the medica as Tavith pushed the stretcher into the palace. Rhain barely took in the wide corridors and arched, ornate ceilings. His boots echoed on the shiny, polished tile as they walked past a row of huge, narrow windows giving a beautiful view of Citadel and her waterfalls and lake.

The medica ward was large and airy, with several rooms located off a central, circular healing area. Tavith pushed the stretcher into position near a trolley filled with medical equipment. Zhalton medicas used a combination of technology and energy manipulation to heal.

Tavith unfastened the woman's dark-blue suit. "These are claw marks."

"A hexid attacked her," Rhain said. "She killed it."

The medica's head whipped up, brow creasing. "She what?"

"She killed it. With a piece of metal from her wrecked ship."

The medica stared at the woman. "Where is she from?"

"A question I want answered." Rhain paused. "After you've healed her, she needs to be restrained."

A scowl bloomed on Tavith's face. "Rhain—"

"I know you don't like it, but she could be dangerous. A trap sent by my father."

The medica released a breath. "Zavir is getting desperate. He wants you to bend."

"I have no intention of bending, and no intention of seeing more of my people die."

The Zhylaw attack on the Renkitis Outpost had been brutal and bloody. The hexids, and another Zhylaw creature called a cupra, had torn the people apart—every man, woman, and child.

A muscle ticked in Rhain's jaw. He saw the dead in his nightmares.

The people he'd failed.

"Rhain." Tavith touched his arm. "Renkitis was not your fault."

"I am the overlord. It is *my* job to protect my planet and her people."

"You do that. Every day. You give more than is sometimes wise. If you push too far..." The medica looked away.

Yes. Rhain was very aware that he had his father's blood in him. If he pushed too far, he'd lose control of that darkness inside. Give in to the power-hungry need to grab for more.

He would *not* turn into his father.

He glanced at the woman, and steeled himself. She'd been fierce awake, but now, she looked vulnerable.

He hardened his heart. "Heal her and then restrain her. Let me know when she's awake. I'll lead the interrogation."

Tavith's blue eyes flared. "You can interrogate her in the morning. Go."

Rhain raised a brow. "Who's the overlord here?"

"In my medica ward, it's me." The old man had no qualms about telling Rhain off.

Rhain shook his head. He'd get his answers in the morning.

MAL WOKE and blinked at the octagonal tile pattern on the white ceiling.

Where the hell was she?

She moved on the bunk. She felt no pain. No aches. She actually felt really rested.

Weird. She was pretty sure the last thing she remembered was pain.

And a big, hot guy with silver eyes.

Wait.

She jerked up to a sitting position, and something wrenched on her left wrist.

What the—?

A glowing band of red energy had her tethered to the side of the bed. She tugged on it and the band tightened until she winced. She stopped moving and the band loosened a little.

Mal looked around, her pulse racing.

It looked like some sort of infirmary. She could see out to several rooms with more empty bunks. Long, elegant windows revealed a sun-drenched sky.

Fuck.

Everything came back to her in a rush.

The fierce creature attacking her.

The crash.

Poppy.

Mal's mouth went dry. She had to find Poppy.

"Hello?" She jerked on the binding again. She slipped off the bunk and realized that she was only wearing her sports bra and panties. Her flight suit was missing.

The floor was smooth stone, but it was warm under her bare feet.

"Don't panic," she whispered. "You're alive. You're going to find Poppy."

She remembered that she'd had a metal shard in her belly, and that damn creature had clawed her.

She touched her stomach.

Nothing. No pain. No marks. No scars.

She yanked on her wrist again. The bunk moved an inch, but the damn energy band tightened again.

"Good, you're awake," a male voice said.

She looked up. The man was older, with dark skin, a round face, and blue, intelligent eyes. His gray hair was buzzed short against his skull. He wore a tunic-style top and trousers in a rich green.

Nearby, she spotted a trolley with some medical equipment on it. She snatched up a long, metal rod and brandished it at the man with her free hand.

"Who the fuck are you, and where am I?"

"Take it easy." The man spoke calmly, and held his hand out like he was placating a wild animal.

"I won't take it easy," she said.

A sudden wave of dizziness hit Mal. She felt a sting in the back of her neck and touched it. There was a bump of a tiny, thin scar.

"That'll heal up shortly," the man said. "I inserted a translator."

"You put something inside me!" She fought back a spurt of panic.

"To allow you to communicate. I'm a medica. A doctor. I'm here to heal, not harm."

"And I'm just supposed to believe you." She yanked on her wrist. "When I'm tied up."

"Yes, well, that wasn't my decision. This is my medica ward and I take care of all my patients."

Her skin itched like crazy, and she wanted to scratch it.

"You must be thirsty," the man said.

"I want to leave."

"You aren't fully healed yet." He stepped closer.

She whipped the tool up. "Don't touch me."

The doctor lifted his hands, nothing but patience on his face.

Then a wave of dizziness made Mal stagger.

"You need more rest. I did what I could, but you have a concussion, as well. And your physiology is new to me." The doctor shrugged. "I'm good, but I'm not a miracle worker. I don't know the baselines for your species yet, but I suspect your vitals are elevated."

Species?

God. None of this mattered. She needed to find Poppy. The room spun sideways, her skin itched even more, and her head throbbed like someone had hit it with a hammer.

Mal gritted her teeth. "I have to go."

Poppy was smart, but if confronted by a giant, snarling beast, she couldn't fight it. She had no killer instinct.

Mal's knees turned to cooked noodles, and she clutched the bed.

The doctor shifted closer. "You're feeling dizzy?"

She only saw concern on the man's face. She gripped the bed to stay upright and nodded. "It doesn't matter. I need to find my friend."

"Friend?"

She nodded. "My ship crashed. I wasn't alone. There was a scientist with me. Dr. Poppy Ellison."

Sympathy crossed the man's face. She hated seeing it, hated the ugly feeling it caused in her gut.

"I'm sorry. From what I hear, your ship was a tangled wreck and there were no other survivors."

No. Mal's gut clenched so hard that she felt sick.

Poppy.

Sorrow swamped her.

"Do you have any other symptoms?" the medica asked.

"My skin is itchy," she said dully. "I have a metallic taste in my mouth." The words felt ripped out of her. She hated showing any weakness.

"I'll run some scans."

She met his gaze. "Where am I?"

"You're in my medica ward, in the royal palace in the city of Citadel. On the planet of Zhalto in the Sarkany System."

All of which meant nothing to her.

"I've never heard of Zhalto." She tugged on her wrist. "And this?"

"Until you're questioned by the overlord, you are to be restrained. We are at war, and there are some fears that you're an enemy agent."

Mal let out a choked laugh. Her test had gone wrong, she'd been flung across the galaxy, and now she'd crash landed in the middle of a war.

Wow. She really couldn't catch a break.

"What's your name?" The man's voice was gentle.

She sighed. "Mallory. Mallory West."

"It's nice to meet you, Mallory. I'm Tavith."

"Ah, thanks for fixing me up."

"That's my pleasure."

"And I go by Mal." She scratched her arm. The itch was getting worse.

"May I scan you? I'd like to help you feel better."

"Sure. Why not?" If he'd wanted to kill her, he would've done it by now.

Tavith touched a band on his wrist, and she watched a blue projection flare up into the air.

"Oh, wow." She stared at the incomprehensible alien writing.

He frowned as he studied it. "Hmm, something is stimulating an immune response from your body." He reached over and grabbed something off the trolley. "Here. This should help."

He pressed the patch to her skin on her arm. It dissolved away. A second later, the itching stopped, and her head cleared.

A warm sensation flowed through her, and she grinned. It felt like she'd knocked back a shot of tequila. "Wow, Doc, that is some potent stuff."

"It's not for a normal Zhalton." He eyed her. "Drink this."

She sipped the clear fluid. It tasted like water.

Slowly, the high sensation faded and left her feeling good, energized. "Tavith, I won't give up on my friend unless I see her body. I made it, so she could have as well."

The doctor frowned. "You need to discuss that with the overlord."

Well, if she was going to meet some alien king, she wanted to be dressed in more than her underwear. "Do you have any clothes I can wear?"

With a nod, the doctor hurried away. She heard him rummaging around in a closet, then he returned, holding some folded clothes. With her arm still tethered, she awkwardly pulled on a pair of loose trousers. Next was a sleeveless, wrap-style shirt that she wrapped around her torso and tied up on the side. Her arm didn't even have to be freed for her to get it on.

"Thank you. I could do with some fresh air." AKA, scope out her surroundings and plan a way out.

The medica nodded. He untethered her arm, leaving the red band around her wrist. She tried to see what he'd done and how it unfastened, but it just seemed to obey his touch.

He led her to a door near the windows. He touched the lock, and she felt a flare of energy. The door shimmered and just disappeared. *Cool.*

Tavith waved her onto a small balcony.

Mal stepped outside and her stomach fell away. "Oh, my God."

Wind tugged at her loose hair. It was a playful breeze, laden with interesting and unusual smells.

The city was set in a tight, circular valley. Glittering, white-stone buildings tumbled down all sides of the mountains, forming a bowl.

It was stunning. Like something from a fairytale. In several places, waterfalls poured downward. Mal moved to the ornate, carved railing and leaned over. A placid, blue lake lay far below. Several bridges crisscrossed between the grand, beautiful buildings. She saw people walking along various terraces, wearing clothes of bright colors with touches of gold, silver, and bronze. From somewhere close by, haunting, beautiful string music floated up to her.

"Welcome to Citadel," Tavith said.

She couldn't form any words. She heard a faint sound and looked up. A red-tinged sun hung overhead, and a second later, a ship appeared.

She sucked in a breath, her lips tilting upward. It had a sleek, central body, with two arched wings. The wings had large circles cut out of them and blue energy crackled in the space. She turned her head, trying to take everything in. A wide, main bridge led up to what she guessed was the palace. A man was walking across it. Several people were with him, some jogging to keep up with his long strides.

He seemed familiar.

Mal's heart skipped a beat or two. One thing was for sure, he was a female fantasy come to life.

He walked like a man in charge. Muscle corded his powerful body. She recognized a fighter—built for strength. He wore black, fitted pants tucked into boots. A fitted black shirt edged with red molded across his broad form. Someone said something to him, and he turned his head.

Wow.

He was close enough that she could take in the strong jaw, sharp blade of his nose, and just enough ruggedness to pique her interest. She'd never been one for pretty boys.

His dark hair was a little long, giving him a masculine, sexy appeal. He was designed to make a female sit up and take notice.

She couldn't see his eyes from here, but she knew that they'd be silver.

It was the man from the crash. She remembered him. She remembered silver eyes brimming with power.

She felt that power throb off him. Even across the distance between them.

He was a man used to being in charge, every order obeyed, who wouldn't be polite or civilized.

The hairs on her arms rose. She felt a strange mix of desire and fear.

"Who's that?" she asked.

"That's the overlord."

Crap. Of course, it was.

Suddenly, the man lifted his head.

His gaze hit hers, ensnared. She couldn't look away from the twisting silver. She felt his power swell around him.

Tavith cleared his throat. "I believe he's on his way to interrogate you."

Yep, she just couldn't catch a break.

CHAPTER FOUR

"Overlord, the nobles are in an uproar over the attacks by the Zhylaw."

Rhain couldn't drag his gaze off the woman standing on the medica ward balcony to look at his advisor.

She stared back, confident, defiant. Was she his father's creature? An assassin or a spy?

He shoved those thoughts away. He'd get his answers soon.

"Jaro, the Houses are always in an uproar over something." They strode off the bridge and through the main doorway into the coolness of the atrium. A soaring, glass-dome ceiling flared overhead. There was a tree in the center, in full bloom.

Nine houses made up the inner circle on Zhalto, and while wealth and holdings counted for a lot, the ability to wield energy was paramount.

The dukes and duchesses and counts and countesses of the powerful Houses all commanded a great deal of ability. Most of Rhain's elite fighters came from the Houses.

"Will you make time to meet with them?" Jaro asked.

Rhain hid his wince. "Yes. If something doesn't come up."

On his other side, Thadd snorted.

The tall, lean Jaro shot the captain a look. "I am well aware the overlord will have a pressing emergency to attend to when the meeting is due to commence."

Rhain kept his face blank. He had a planet to protect, and listening to the nobles argue and complain, didn't help him do that.

Jaro released a breath, pushing his long, brown hair back. "The long-range scouts are back with new intel on the Zhylaw."

Now Rhain straightened. He'd been waiting to hear from the scouts. "Good, Jaro. Tell me."

"They've tracked the invaders to the heart of the Barrens," Jaro said. "They definitely have a base there, although we aren't sure where exactly."

Of course, they did. The Barrens were rocky, dangerous, and filled with deadly creatures twisted by the radiation of the Radiance. It was the perfect hiding place.

"The scouts were also able to identify the Zhylaw leader in charge." Jaro paused.

Rhain swiveled. *Finally.* If he knew who was leading his father's attacks, Rhain could better plan his own counterattacks. "Who?"

The normally efficient Jaro fidgeted.

"Jaro?" Rhain growled.

"It's Krastin, my lord."

Rhain's world stopped. *Krastin.*

He looked at his boots, fighting back the rage and pain. Thadd gripped his arm and squeezed.

Krastin was a ruthless, vicious murderer who'd killed Rhain's mother over a decade ago.

He dragged in a breath. Years ago, Zavir had ordered her assassination, and Krastin had been an up-and-coming killer, out to make a name for himself.

"I need to inform my brothers."

"Several Sarkan advisors were also spotted with the Zhylaw warlord," Jaro continued. "They are some of your father's inner circle."

"Call him Zavir." Rhain preferred not to think of the man as his father.

His advisor bowed his head. "Of course, Overlord."

"Thank you, Jaro."

With a nod, the man hurried off.

Thadd eyed Rhain's face.

Rhain sighed. "Don't worry, I'm not going to lose it and charge after Krastin without any thought or planning." But he did want to smash Krastin's face to meat.

"Tavith sent reluctant word that the woman is awake and ready for questioning," Thadd said.

Rhain wanted answers more than ever, but gritted his teeth. "She'll wait. I need to contact my brothers."

His captain nodded.

The two of them strode toward the communication room. People hurried out of Rhain's way. Usually, he took time to talk with his people, but he didn't have it in him today.

He entered the communication chamber and stood in

the center of the empty space. There was no furniture, just pretty mosaic stone walls and a gently curved floor. All designed with the optimum flow of energy in mind.

He calmed his mind as much as he could and pulled the energy to him.

Blue lights flared around the edge of the chamber, then projected upward in front of him.

"Are you all right?" Thadd asked.

"Is that a polite way of saying I'm being a *gorr*?"

Thadd crossed his arms over his chest. "You seem on edge."

"I want to kill Krastin." Rhain's voice was a lethal blade.

"I know."

"And you know I met with some of the families of the dead from the Renkitis Outpost earlier."

"I know."

Yes, Thadd had stood guard, as he always did. He'd seen the grief-stricken relatives.

"I can handle the tears and grief." A king had to. It was part of his duty. "But it was the families with no bodies to burn under the auroras that got to me."

It was a time-honored tradition to burn the dead under the glow of the auroras and set their energy free, back to the flow.

"The *gorr*-cursed Zhylaw," Thadd bit out.

Yes, they'd seen the blood at the outpost. Zhaltons were dead, but the Zhylaw had taken their bodies to do who knew what with them. They would likely turn them into undead monstrosities.

The light projection changed.

A strong face with a hard jaw and rugged lines appeared. The man was slightly in profile and his long, silver-white hair was tied at the base of his neck.

"Rhain," the man's deep voice rumbled through the room.

"Brodin."

His brother was big and strong, and had a wild edge. All Damari did, but as the planet's emperor, Brodin exuded it from his pores. He was powerfully built, unstoppable in battle, and ruled his wild and dangerous people with a fair but iron fist.

He could also shift into a giant damar-wolf.

"My scouts sent word," Rhain said. "It is the warlord Krastin leading the raids here on Zhalto."

Brodin cursed. "That ass is a boil that needs lancing, Rhain."

"You've dealt with him before?"

"Once. He attacked some of our exploration ships on the edge of the system." Brodin's scowl said it all.

"You know he killed my mother."

Brodin bowed his head. "I know. He needs to die, and this is your chance for retribution. Krastin isn't subtle in his attacks and there is no line he won't cross."

There was disdain in Brodin's voice, and that was saying something. Brodin could shapeshift into a giant wolf, and wielded a deadly axe on the battlefield.

"He has little skill or strategy. He's like a wrecking machine, crashing through, throwing his fighters and beasts everywhere. He treats them as expendable."

The screen blinked and their other brother appeared.

Lean, intense, with gold eyes in a sharp, intense face; his dark hair was clipped short.

"Hello, Graylan," Rhain said.

"Rhain. How are you holding up?"

His other brother had a low voice that held a hint of menace. The kind of voice that made the hairs on the back of one's neck rise.

"Zavir is nipping at my people, outposts, convoys. Taking their lives and leaving no bodies. We have hexids everywhere."

And Zavir would never stop. All three of them knew it.

"I've heard the reports," his brother replied.

"I was telling Brodin that we've identified Krastin as the warlord our father sent here. He's holed up somewhere in the Barrens."

"I've heard of him," Graylan said darkly. "And I know it must be difficult for you."

"My mother died a long time ago, but I want justice for her." When she'd been murdered, he'd been a young, hot-tempered man just out of his teenage years. He'd wanted to hunt Krastin down then.

But the nobles had demanded he stay. He'd been the new overlord, his duty to the planet, and calming the people after the death of the queen. The dukes and counts had harassed him until he'd agreed not to leave.

"Do you need assistance?" Brodin asked. "I can send some of my cleavers."

"Not yet." It was a generous offer. Brodin's cleavers were his elite shapeshifters—deadly with both weapons and claws. "I will hunt Krastin down. No matter what."

And send a blunt message to their father. "I wanted to warn you both. He sent Krastin here, and he may send warlords to your planet as well."

Graylan scowled and nodded.

Brodin pulled in a breath. "I've had reports. Sightings of foreigners on Damar. We've had people who've gone missing while out hunting."

"Track them down, Brodin. If the Zhylaw are involved, they'll flood you with their rotten creatures."

Face grim, Rhain's brother nodded.

"Now, I have to go," Rhain said. "We have a suspected agent of Zavir's in custody. I need to question her."

"Good luck, brother," Brodin said.

Graylan nodded.

The projection winked out.

Rhain released a breath. "My father won't stop, Thadd. He's ruthless, power-hungry. He wants me and my brothers, not for us, not for any love for his sons, but for our power."

"Yes. The Sarkans have always been bloodthirsty, and Zavir is the pinnacle of that. Anything to advance the wealth and might of Sarkan."

"Let's see what our unexpected guest has to say."

Rhain strode up the stairs to the medica ward, Thadd a menacing shadow at his side. He lifted a hand and, with a pulse of energy, the medica ward doors flew open.

Tavith spun from the bench where he stood. "Why don't you just tear them off the hinges?"

Rhain ignored the sarcasm. There were very few

people he let speak to him like this, but Tavith had known him since he was a child. "Where is she?"

"In the main examination room." Tavith nodded to a doorway. "As requested."

Rhain felt the medica's disapproval. "She might be a spy, a weapon sent from Sarkan."

"You don't know that. I feel like you've already made up your mind."

"I'm not going to hurt her."

Yet. The darkness twisted inside him. If she proved a danger to his people...

Tavith waved a hand, annoyance stamped on his dark features. "She's not fully healed. I'm running scans because she's still showing some symptoms, which I suspect is her body reacting to our environment."

Rhain turned and held a hand up to the examination room door. It shimmered open.

The woman sat on a chair, one wrist tied to the side of it with an energy band.

Her head lifted.

"Ah, the boss man has arrived."

Thadd stayed outside and out of sight, but Rhain knew his captain was ready to intervene at any second.

She jerked her bound wrist. "Your hospitality is a little lacking." Her strange green gold eyes sparked. "What gives you the right to take an injured woman and tie her up?"

"I am the overlord."

"Oh, so what you say goes? You can do whatever you want? Sounds like a dictator to me."

Rhain scowled at her. His father was a dictator, not him. "I don't want to hurt you."

"Then let me go." She shot a pointed look at her wrist.

"I can't do that."

"I need to get out of here and search for my friend."

Rhain narrowed his gaze. *Friend?* There'd been no one else in the wreckage. Just a lie to get herself free.

"I have questions and I expect you to answer them."

The woman's chin lifted. "Not going to happen. Do your worst, but remember, you aren't my damn overlord."

THE ITCHINESS and dizziness were back with a vengeance.

Mal shifted on the chair, and felt a trickle of perspiration. She refused to show her discomfort.

They'd been at it for a while now.

The silver-eyed king growled questions at her and she told him to shove it.

"Tell me what your mission is." The overlord seemed a little ticked. He was losing his patience.

Good. "My mission was to test my new ship. Something went wrong and we crashed. I need to get out of here and find the woman who was with me."

"No one was with you."

"Her part of the ship must've crashed somewhere else. I *need* to find her."

Something moved in his silver eyes.

"You know something." Mal's pulse skittered.

The overlord shook his head. "If she crashed, she's likely dead."

Mal jerked. "I survived, so she could have as well."

"Even if she survived the crash, she'd be in the Barrens. It's wild and dangerous there."

Mal's stomach turned. "I won't give up on her."

"*Gorr*, you're stubborn."

"I don't know what *gorr* means, but right back at you," she spat.

"It's just a curse word. No one remembers where it came from." He sucked in a breath. "Tell me your name, where you're from, and your mission."

"I'm from Vulcan," she said. "No, Tatooine."

He shook his head. "Tell me."

"Screw you."

He closed his eyes, and joined his hands together in front of him, like he was praying.

What now? Mal felt the air charge. It was like static electricity before a storm. Energy skittered over her skin, making the itching worse.

"Tell me what I want to know," his voice was deeper, more resonant.

He was doing something. She felt a heavy pressure start to bear down on her. The energy was pushing against her, squeezing.

"No," she pushed out between her gritted teeth. She saw a red glow on his hands and her heart squeezed. "What...are you doing?"

"Pulling energy from my planet's magnetic field. Zhaltons have evolved to be able to manipulate and use it."

"What?" she breathed.

"Don't pretend you don't know."

"I don't," she bit out.

"Answer my questions."

The pressure was starting to hurt. She felt like she was caught in a vise. She imagined shoving the pressure away, flinging it off her like an old coat.

Suddenly, it eased and she saw the overlord stiffen. His gaze narrowed on her.

"I'm not your enemy, Overlord."

He dragged a chair over in front of her and dropped into it. He looked a little tired.

Ha, take that scary, handsome, alien king.

He scraped a hand through his dark hair. "You have a strong will."

"My stepfather used to say I had a head like a lump of rock."

A flare of amusement in those silver eyes. "I concur."

"Ha-ha."

"What's your name?"

"You first," she countered.

He was silent for a moment. "Overlord Rhain Zhalto Sarkany, ruler of the planet Zhalto."

"Wow, that is a mouthful."

He looked exasperated. "Rhain, woman. My name is Rhain."

"I'm Mal. Mallory West, but I prefer Mal. And all I want to do is find my friend, Dr. Poppy Ellison. She's a scientist, not a—"

"A warrior like you."

Mal shrugged. "I can fight, but I'm actually a pilot."

"What I see is a perfectly designed trap. Female, injured, and destined to stab me in the back."

She huffed out a breath. "I kind of do want to stab you. Maybe in the eye. Look, surely you saw that my ship isn't from your planet?"

"My enemy is smart and cunning. He could've planned that."

"Who is this bad guy I'm supposedly working for?"

"My father."

"Ah." She sank back in her chair. "Daddy problems are the worst."

A muscle ticked in Rhain's jaw. "My father is a powerful warmonger."

"Yikes. I never knew mine, but my mother met a good man when I was little. After she died, he raised me." Grief hit her. She wished Rusty was here. He always had good, gruff advice.

"You grieve for him?"

Her head snapped up and she looked at Rhain. "Yes. He died recently."

The king cocked his handsome, rugged face. Power emanated off him, and she saw it shifting in his eyes. "You pushed off my power before. You have some Zhalton abilities."

"I have no idea what you're talking about. I just wanted you to stop whatever the hell you were doing."

He leaned closer and she picked up his scent. He smelled vaguely like something woody, with a touch of fresh pine.

Great, her captor looked good *and* smelled good. Lucky her.

"I can't take the risk, Mallory West. Zavir, my father, keeps sending his creatures to kill my people."

"Like that beast I fought?"

"It's called a hexid."

"Hexid. It smelled...wrong."

"Yes, they are created by the Zhylaw. My father's allies. They use technology to corrupt different creatures and expand their lives."

"Expand? You mean they're dead?" She grimaced.

"Mostly. They're holding onto life by a thread, but they are mostly mindless. They follow orders but when not controlled, they hunt and attack wildly."

Mal ran a hand over her head. "And if these creatures slipped the Zhylaw's leashes?"

"They'd become ravenous killers. Just a few are able to take down hundreds of fighters in a bloodbath."

Shit. Mal released a breath. "I want nothing to do with that. I just want to find Poppy and then find a way home."

Rhain paused for a moment. "A second larger bit of debris fell in the Badus Mountains."

Mal straightened. "You asshole. She could be hurt—"

"The Badus Mountains are filled with lava pools, geysers, noxious gases, wild beasts."

"I don't care!"

"It is also the heart of where the hexids are coming from."

Goddammit. "They have a base there."

He nodded. "My father sent a dangerous warlord here. His name is Krastin."

"I have to go."

Rhain steeled himself. "Admit you work for Zavir, and tell me your mission."

"No!" she jerked in her chair. "You know I have nothing to do with your asshole father. Let. Me. Go." She gritted her teeth together to stop a scream of frustration. Dizziness swamped her.

Suddenly, a window shattered. *What the hell?*

Rhain studied it, his brow creased.

She blinked. She hadn't done that. *Right?*

"I can't take the risk of freeing you, Mal. We have too many unanswered questions."

"*Argh.*" She jerked on the binding. It tightened, her fingers going numb.

Rhain rose.

Even spitting mad, she took a second to admire that powerful body, the strong thighs, the flat stomach, and the muscled arms.

Quit noticing what he looks like, Mal.

"Tell Tavith when you're ready to talk." Rhain strode out, shooting her one last unreadable look.

Asshole.

Mal slumped back against the chair and the energy band loosened. The feeling rushed back into her fingers.

She looked at the window and her vision blurred a little. Her skin felt like it was on fire.

Ugh. She needed a decent night's sleep. She could hardly help Poppy if she couldn't even walk. Mal blew out a breath. How the hell was she going to get away from Rhain, who could wield energy with a wave of a hand? Could all Zhaltons use it?

She fought back her skitter of unease. It didn't

matter. She wouldn't let anything stop her from finding Poppy. As Rusty had always told her, courage was being scared to death, but saddling up anyway.

Tomorrow. Tomorrow, she'd wait for her chance to escape. She had to find the Badus Mountains.

Hold on, Poppy. I'm coming soon.

CHAPTER FIVE

Rhain sank back in his chair at the large table. It was crafted from a hunk of polished black rock from the Emerys Gorges in the southern reaches of Zhalto.

The Duke of Jadirel was droning on about the security of his farms. Across the table, the Count of Bentlae looked ready to launch across the polished surface and argue. Both men loved to contradict each other, bicker, and outbid each other on business deals. It stemmed from a centuries-old feud over a stolen bride.

Shifting, Rhain caught the gaze of the Countess of Naveri. She winked.

Thadd's mother was a formidable, handsome woman who wasn't afraid of anything or anyone. She freely shared her opinion and waded into arguments between the Houses when it suited her. She'd been his mother's best friend, and treated Rhain like a second son, especially after his mother had died.

"Enough." Rhain didn't thump his fist on the table,

but his voice was enough to have the nobles cut off mid-sentence. He was so tired and just wanted some quiet.

Between the Renkitis Outpost attack, fighting the hexids, and his stubborn captive, he was running low on patience and energy.

"We will stop at nothing to hunt down Krastin and stop his army of beasts. They are not welcome here and I will not let them hurt anymore of my people." Rhain leaned forward. "I care about your farms and holdings, but I care more about lives. Krastin will pay for our dead." He scanned the room. "My fighters are committed, and I expect aid from all of you if and when it is required."

There were murmurs and nods. The Duke of Jadirel's mouth flattened, but he gave a decisive nod. The Houses might squabble, but at the end of the day, they were all Zhalton.

"Dismissed," Rhain said.

The nobles all rose and swept out.

The countess came to him and cupped his cheeks. "You look tired, my boy."

He'd always be a boy to Daneris Naveri, as would Thadd. "It's been a long day."

"You visited the families of the Renkitis Outpost victims." She patted his cheek, sympathy on her face. "And I hear that you have a prisoner. One of Zavir's spies."

As always, Daneris had her sources. "She claims that she isn't, but she isn't answering my questions. I'll interrogate her again in the morning."

When he rose, the countess slid her arm through his.

As they walked out of the meeting chamber, the skirts of her long, gold dress swished.

"You need a queen."

Rhain gave a mental groan. The countess was determined to get Rhain or Thadd married off. She wanted grandbabies to spoil outrageously.

"I don't have time," he said.

"Not a pretty court jewel. Someone who can share the burden of ruling with you."

Rhain had yet to meet any woman like that.

Daneris stopped, smiled. "I know you're ignoring my suggestion."

Despite his tiredness, he smiled back. "Never."

The countess rolled her bright-blue eyes, then she glanced out the windows. Auroras filled the night sky with color. Tonight, they were extra bright and vibrant, dancing wildly. He watched the blue-green colors shift and flow like a river in flood.

"The energy is especially strong tonight," she said. "Do you feel it?"

He nodded. Sometimes the magnetic field was fully charged by strong solar winds from the sun. He felt the energy tingle on his skin, in his gut.

"They say that's good luck," she said. "That the auroras are smiling down at us. Go and get some sleep, Rhain."

He kissed her cheek. "No woman could ever compare to you."

Pleasure filled her face. "Off with you. And Rhain, your mother would be so proud of you."

His throat tightened.

Back in his bedroom suite, he managed a quick shower before he fell into his big bed naked. Sleep claimed him in seconds.

He didn't expect to dream.

He felt fingers stroke his bicep, then splay across his chest.

"Hard as steel," a female voice muttered. "Guessed as much."

Rhain raised his brows, taking a second to savor the firm touch.

The fingers stroked his pecs. "It's a hell of a chest."

Then he opened his eyes and saw Mallory West leaning over him.

He was flat on his back on lush grass, and strangely he was wearing traditional Zhalton battle gear: a battle skirt, huge belt around his waist, and a leather harness across his bare chest, with his royal medallion—worn by Zhalton's rulers for centuries—set on it. His swords were in sheaths by his hips, when usually he wore them on his back. He only wore traditional dress for ceremonies and events.

Energy permeated everything, and he felt it wash over his skin.

"Like what you see?" he drawled.

The hand on him stilled. Her eyes shot wide. "Hey, this is my dream. No talking. You annoy me when you talk."

"Well, this is my dream too."

Her nose wrinkled and she snatched her hand back.

Missing her touch, he grabbed her hand and sat up.

She had strong, long fingers. He easily pictured them on a sword, on the controls of a ship, or on his skin.

Gorr. He had no business being tantalized by his captive, a possible enemy spy.

"The energy is up tonight," he said. "It's been known to link people's dreams." Although usually people who were strongly connected—lovers, partners, family.

"Energy?" She frowned.

"Yes, from the magnetic field. Zhalto has a very strong one due to the composition of the planet's core."

"Ah, that explains the auroras." She glanced at the night sky above them. "And the whole being able to use energy with your bare hands."

He inclined his head.

"Can you use the abilities when you're off the planet?"

"Not always. It depends on the magnetic field of the planets I visit." Being off Zhalto always felt like having his senses dulled. It was vaguely uncomfortable.

It was partly why Zhaltons were warriors. They trained daily with their weapons, knowing if they were off the planet, they couldn't rely on their energy abilities.

Mal pushed to her feet and Rhain did the same.

She wore strange clothes—fitted pants made of a heavy, blue-stained fabric that shaped her long legs and a tight, black, sleeveless shirt that showed off toned arms and a hint of high, firm breasts. Her brown hair was loose, a gentle breeze making it dance around her shoulders.

They stood in a flower field covered in a carpet of red larka flowers.

"Your planet sure is pretty," she said.

"It is. And I'll protect it from my father with everything I have."

"Loyalty and dedication." She lifted her chin. "I feel the same way about finding my friend, Poppy. I won't give up on her."

Rhain noted the stubborn tilt to Mal's jaw. He suspected she never made anything easy.

"It is highly likely that your friend didn't survive," he said gently.

"Don't say that!"

"I only speak the truth—"

She rushed him.

The punch slammed into his gut. With a grunt, he knocked her arm away. She tried to knee him, and he bumped her leg aside. She was strong.

The next thing he knew, her foot was flying at his face.

With a growl, Rhain ducked, then tackled her to the ground. He landed on top of her, pinning her in place.

"Ugh, you weigh a ton." She bucked.

"Quit fighting." He managed to pin her arms above her head.

"No." She renewed her struggles.

And Rhain's body took note of the strong, enticing, very female one squirming beneath him.

"Mal," he ground out. "Stop."

Something in his tone got through because she stilled. Her gaze locked on his face. His skimmed over hers, taking in the intriguing scar bisecting her eyebrow—he wanted to know how she'd gotten it—and the tiny black mark on her cheekbone. That one he wanted to kiss.

He saw awareness flicker in her gaze and she sucked in a breath, pushing her breasts against his chest.

They both groaned.

Then suddenly, a low, feral growl cut through the night.

Rhain whipped his head up.

A large hexid was creeping toward them.

Swallowing a curse, Rhain leaped to his feet.

Mal rolled. "Not another one."

Rhain drew his swords. The hexid paused, black eyes staring like fathomless black holes, sucking all light in.

"Oh, man, those swords are pure beauty," Mal said.

He heard reverence in her voice as she eyed his weapons covetously.

"They were designed for me. They're kilwar blades."

"Incredible craftsmanship."

Rhain turned his wrist and held one out to her.

She gripped the hilt. "It's too heavy for me to use for very long, but it isn't as heavy as I expected." She sliced it through the air, her gaze shifting to the crouched hexid.

Two more hexids appeared out of the darkness.

Gorr. He didn't need hexids in his dreams as well.

Rhain lifted his sword and charged it with energy. Lights on the kilwar lit up, glowing red.

"Wow." Mal's brows winged up. "You'll have to show me how to do that."

"You need to be Zhalton, unfortunately. We can charge our weapons with energy."

"Oh, well, guess I'll have to make do." She lifted the sword.

The hexids charged.

Rhain leaped, his sword raised. He sliced at the lead beast and black blood sprayed.

Beside him, Mal wielded his second kilwar with shocking skill. Her style was different, but no less effective. She slid low and stabbed the hexid in the gut. It bellowed and she yanked the blade free and sliced through its thighs.

Auroras above, she could fight.

He was distracted by Mal, so he didn't see the third hexid until it slammed into him.

It might be a dream, but he still felt the sting of claws raking him. The pain felt very real. The beast took him to the ground, pinning his sword under one giant claw.

Suddenly, a kilwar sliced along the hexid's side. Mal let out a cry and reversed direction, opening up a wicked gash on the hexid's body. With a pained yelp, it leaped off Rhain.

He took Mal's outstretched hand and jumped up.

"Okay?" she asked, her gaze on the injured hexid.

"Yes." Thanks to her.

Around them, more hexids blinked into existence.

"Our shared dream sucks," Mal said.

Rhain pulled in a breath and lifted his sword. "It started off fine."

Mal grinned. "You ready to fight, your Overlordness?"

The way she twisted his title, with a hint of teasing, should have annoyed him. They moved, pressing their backs together.

"I'm ready," he said.

The hexids attacked.

Rhain's and Mal's swords sliced and slashed.

They spun, twirled, and lunged, working together in perfect synchronicity as they cut down beast after beast.

Whenever he stepped back, she was there, moving forward.

He hacked into a large hexid, and heard Mal grunt, taking down another one. Thick, black blood stained the grass.

Finally, he lowered his sword, his chest heaving.

All the hexids were dead.

With the auroras dancing overhead, he turned.

Mal grinned. "You know how to show a girl a good time, Overlord."

He smiled back. His gut was hot, his blood heated. All he could see was her.

He strode toward her. Her grin faded, leaving only plain desire on her face. He slid his free arm around her, hauling her close. Then he wasn't sure who moved first, her or him.

Their mouths collided.

Rhain deepened the kiss, desperate for the taste of her, for more of her.

Then he blinked and she was gone.

His eyes snapped open. He was lying alone in his bed in his shadowed room, arms empty and cock hard.

The auroras danced outside and he tasted the spice of Mal on his lips.

MAL SAT in her chair and glared at the goddamned band on her wrist.

She'd been fiddling with the stupid thing all morning and was no closer to working out how to get free. She growled. Tavith had brought her a tray of weird food for lunch—some of which had been a salad made of flowers. The doctor had assured her they were edible and nutritious.

She had no interest in eating flowers. She'd kill for a steak.

She dropped back in the chair. There had been no sign of his Overlordness. Clearly, he'd had better things to do today.

Mal was actually glad.

She'd had the craziest dream during the night. Of touching Rhain, fighting beside him with one of his super-cool swords, and then kissing his brains out.

Crossing her legs, she squeezed her thighs together, a little embarrassed that she was totally turned on. She heaved out a breath. Having sex dreams about her alien captor was probably a really bad idea.

She really needed to get out of there.

She looked at the dreaded band again. It glowed red. Mocking her.

She'd tugged it, yanked it, tried to cut it, stretch it. Nothing. The more she did anything, the more it tightened.

Her gaze narrowed. *Hmm.* She relaxed, letting her body go lax. She imagined lying on a pristine beach, the sun warm on her skin. She closed her eyes. In the distance, she saw a man walking toward her. His chest was bare, his dark, shaggy hair framing his rugged face.

Rhain.

Get out of my daydream. Damn, she couldn't escape him.

Dragging in a breath, she pictured her *empty* beach. Then totally calm, she touched the band and imagined it releasing.

The band began to heat and the hairs on her arms rose. It was growing hot enough to burn her skin.

Ow, ow. Oh, shit.

Then it fell off.

Mal blinked. She rubbed her wrist and smiled. *Hot damn.* Finally, a break.

Quietly, she moved to the open door to the balcony. Tavith had opened it earlier to give her some fresh air. She slipped outside. The afternoon sun hung in the sky, heading toward the distant horizon.

One of those cool flyers moved overhead. It was near soundless, just making a slight buzzing noise. She watched the shimmer of energy within the huge circles in the wings.

She'd kill to sit in one and get her hands on the controls.

Mal shook her head. Right now, she needed to get out of this palace. Her plan was to find some shoes, supplies, and a weapon.

And find out how to get to the Badus Mountains.

She peered over the balcony railing. The buildings were made of smooth, white stone, but there were several ornate elements that stuck out, forming convenient handholds.

Her dizziness wasn't too bad at the moment, thankfully. Guess it was time for a climb.

She swung her leg over the railing, and maneuvered so she was pressed flat against the wall. She started to climb down. Hopefully no one spotted her.

Nothing to see here, move along.

Mal shifted carefully, then glanced down. Multiple terrace levels below formed the city. But then she made the mistake of looking all the way down to the lake.

The blue, flat water was *really* far down. Her stomach turned. She was a pilot. She didn't mind heights… From the safety of a cockpit.

"Suck it up, Mal," she muttered.

She focused on the rock wall and kept moving downward.

She heard voices, laughter. The citizens of Citadel going about their business.

But what about Poppy? Where was she? Was she hurt?

Mal's jaw tightened and suddenly her foot slid off its foothold. She gripped hard, and waited a second until she found her balance. She shifted her weight and kept climbing.

But a moment later, her fingers slipped off a handhold.

Oh, shit.

Mal slid down the wall, and then hit the ground on her ass—hard.

Her bones rattled. *Ow.*

A few people on the open terrace stopped to look at her, faces puzzled.

"I'm fine." She rose. "Absolutely fine. Nothing to see here." She dusted herself off.

She strode down the terrace, trying to blend in. Shops lined one side, while the other was a stunning view of the center of the city with its waterfalls and bridges, and down to the lake.

The inhabitants' clothing was fairly simple and streamlined—fitted trousers, tunic-like tops, or shirts that wrapped and tied on—but Zhaltons clearly liked color. All shades of the rainbow were present, from the brightest red to eye-searing yellow.

She passed stalls selling what looked like fruits—most appearing weird and wonderful. Others sold flowers in a multitude of colors and shapes. Strangely, she felt the hum of energy off some of them. There were also spices, in large, fragrant, colorful piles. Another stall sold musical instruments.

Oh, she really wanted to touch them. Mal played the guitar, and she wasn't too bad. This stall had a stand of what looked like flutes, and some beautifully carved wooden instruments, a few that looked guitar-like.

No time, Mal. She turned away and breathed deep. The city of Citadel smelled gorgeous.

But she didn't have time to appreciate the beauty. She turned and darted down a narrow alley. Buildings rose up around her, and clothes fluttered on lines anchored from various windows.

Hmm. On one lower line, she spotted some leather pants that looked about her size in a supple brown. There was also a blue shirt on another line, with a glint of silver at the neckline.

She leaped up and deftly nabbed them, and kept walking, tucking the garments under her arm.

She followed the twists and turns of the alleyways. She passed some older men and women playing some sort of projected game above a board that looked vaguely like a chess board. As she walked past another doorway, she nabbed a pair of black boots that were resting on a mat.

She passed a junction and watched kids running and chasing each other, giggling loudly. She carefully slipped into an alcove, and changed into the clothes. She shimmied into the pants. The boots were a little big, but they'd do.

She wrapped her hair up in a bun on top of her head and she slipped out. The kids were still playing, and the sight of it made her lips curve briefly in a smile. She heard music and spotted a middle-aged woman sitting on a stoop, playing a stringed instrument. Her eyes were closed, lost in making the beautiful music. Mal watched her for a moment, noting how she held it against her slim shoulder and how she plucked the strings.

With regret, Mal forced herself to keep moving. She came to a flower stall and stopped by to sniff one. It smelled divine.

An older, weathered man stepped around the display and smiled at her. He nabbed a red bloom from the display and handed it to her.

"Oh, I can't pay," Mal said.

"No worries. A pretty flower for a pretty woman."

She took it and smiled. "Thank you. It's beautiful."

"You look like you needed some kindness."

Mal felt a little kick under her heart. "Things have been a little rough lately." She tucked the flower behind her ear. "Thanks again."

The man inclined his head. "Be well."

Suddenly, the kids got noisier, excitement ringing in their voices. "Palace guards are headed this way!"

Shit. Mal forced herself to stay relaxed and slipped into a doorway.

Two tall, brawny guards wearing red sashes walked past. They strode with purpose.

Crap. Were they looking for her?

She needed a weapon, and then to get out of the city.

The guards turned a corner and were gone. She stepped out and approached the kids.

"Hey, have you guys heard of the Badus Mountains?"

They blinked at her.

"Yeah," one said.

Another one shrugged. "Everyone has."

"My mother threatens to send me there whenever I disobey her." The boy winced. "Or when I break something."

"How do you get there?" Mal asked.

The oldest of the kids eyed her with suspicious blue eyes. "You're not from around here?"

"No, I'm...from the north."

The kids nodded.

"I've a cousin in Krish," one boy said.

Mal nodded in reply. Wherever that was.

"The Badus Mountains are in the Barrens," the tall kid said. "It's dangerous."

"Right. The Barrens are in which direction?"

They all frowned at her.

"Everyone on Zhalto knows where the Barrens are." The kid's frown deepened.

"I know, I just don't know my way out of Citadel. Refresh my memory."

"The Barrens cut across the center of the planet," the older kid said. "Caused by the Radiance."

"The Radiance." *What was that?*

The boy's brow creased. "The giant solar flare that hit the system centuries ago."

"Right. Of course."

"It sent a blast of radiation like a missile across Zhalto and formed the Barrens," another kid parroted, like he was reading from a script. "It left Zhalto changed forever." The kid wrinkled his nose. "I had to do an assignment on it at school. After that, the magnetic field became stronger, charged with particles from the sun, and Zhaltons adapted."

"I knew that." She remembered vividly how Rhain's blade had lit up during her dream. Hell, could all the Zhaltons use energy like that? If so, she was in trouble.

"So, to get to the Barrens?" she prompted.

"East," the older kid said. "Until the farmland gives way to rocks. The Badus Mountains have a large peak in the center. Mount Yos."

"Great. Thanks, kids."

Mal turned and strode back down the alley. She ended up back out on one of the wide terraces.

Next up, she needed a weapon. She turned a corner and finally the universe stopped being a bitch.

She saw a line of shops with racks of weapons out front. There were swords, axes, knives, crossbows. They were really like nothing she'd seen on Earth. They were exquisite, with different designs, most of them jagged and ornate.

"Best weapons in Citadel." A hard-eyed woman leaned against the weapons racks.

"They look great," Mal said.

"Ahron Weapons specializes in the best charged weapons in all of Zhalto."

Charged weapons? Mal nodded. "I'm just looking."

She wandered farther down the line of shops.

Then she saw it. A gorgeous, simple blade. A saber—solid and strong.

The blade was almost white, the hilt sturdy with a few ornate flourishes. Her hands itched to touch it. She glanced around. She hated stealing, but this was life or death.

Muttering a quiet apology to the seller, she snatched the sword up, then grabbed a scabbard from the display beside her. She nabbed a knife from a nearby table, as well. She spun away and walked quickly. She expected to hear shouts, see someone chasing her down.

Nothing.

In a shadowed corner, she lifted the sword and assessed the weight. Nice. She pulled the scabbard on, and it fit nicely over her back. She fastened it and slid the sword into it.

Right. Now to get out of the city and go east.

Suddenly, the air charged around her, making her skin tingle. She stilled and turned.

Uh-oh.

She spotted Rhain in the distance, striding down the terrace.

People stared at him and stumbled out of his way. Mal felt the rush of energy, like an impending thunderstorm, brewing.

His gaze locked on her.

Mal decided to implement her very clever escape plan.

She turned and ran.

CHAPTER SIX

Rhain saw his escaped prisoner and broke into a sprint.

"Rhain!" Thadd bellowed behind him.

He watched Mal turn into an alley and gave chase. She was fast.

He pulled energy to him and picked up speed.

The alley opened into a small plaza. There were several restaurants, with people seated outside. Nearby, a man was pushing a mobile food cart.

"Get your fresh-baked olver," the man called.

Mal dodged around the cart on those long legs of hers.

Rhain raised a hand. A row of potted plants outside a café lifted into the air. He jerked his hand to the side.

They flew toward Mal.

She dodged the first two, then pulled a sword and slashed at the third.

The pots broke into shards on the ground.

She looked back at him, a jaunty, red flower tucked behind her ear. She smiled, then took off again.

Rhain ran. He used a pulse of energy, and sailed into the air and over the food cart. He heard exclamations from the people nearby.

"You can't escape, Mal," he yelled.

"Watch me!" she yelled back.

She took a hard left and disappeared down another alley. Rhain sprinted down the alley and ran out the other side into a large crowd of people. He swiveled, searching for her dark hair.

There. She disappeared down another narrow street.

This one was filled with colorful fabrics hanging out to dry. It looked like they'd been recently dyed.

He couldn't hear any movement. He pushed past one, then another. All he heard was the fluttering of fabric in the breeze.

She was close, he could feel her.

He paused.

He let the energy pool around him. *Where are you?*

He dodged to the left, brushed a body, and heard a feminine curse. There she was, hiding behind some electric-blue fabric.

She punched him, and he deflected the blow. She twisted and they both turned and ended up wrapped up in a roll of rich, red fabric.

Her face was not far from his and she glared up at him.

"You shouldn't have escaped," he said.

"I'm leaving. I'm not trying to spy or assassinate you."

"Come back and answer my questions."

She cocked her head. "Let me think? No."

Rhain felt a prick at his abdomen.

She had a knife pressed against his gut.

He shook his head. He knew deep down that she wouldn't cut him.

"Are you going to stab me?" he asked.

"Don't push your luck, your Overlordness."

Gorr, that snotty, irreverent tone got to him. "You forget who you're talking to."

"No, I haven't. My arrogant captor who is trying to lock me up." She jabbed the knife a little deeper.

Their faces were close and he saw her gaze drop to his mouth.

"Remembering the kiss in our dream?" he asked.

She sucked in a breath. "No. That was just a dream."

He smiled. "You liked my kilwar blade a lot. And my chest."

Her mouth dropped opened. "That's not...possible."

"Put the knife down. We'll talk." Rhain yanked her closer and absorbed the sting of the blade.

"You idiot," she snapped. "I've cut you."

"It's fine."

She shook her head. "Sorry, no can do."

She shifted the knife to the side and sliced down the side of the fabric. She slipped free. Cursing, Rhain followed.

To find another sheet thrown at him, covering his head.

Gorr. He let loose a pulse of energy and threw the sheet off him. It fluttered up into the air.

He saw Mal disappear at the end of the alley.

Cursing ripely, he ran after her. He spotted her heading back toward the central terrace.

When he reached the terrace, she'd disappeared into the crowd again. He took a few steps and spotted a crumpled red flower on the ground.

Where are you? He stood still and calmed his mind. He felt the pull of the energy field around him.

"Rhain?" Thadd's heavy footsteps sounded behind him.

Rhain felt the solid, strong, life force of his captain.

"She's here." He sensed her, like a bright spark.

The fact she'd escaped and ran, would prove to most that she was the enemy. The nobles would scream for her to be locked up. He had to find her.

"I spoke to some children," Thadd said. "She talked with them."

Rhain heard the reluctance to share in Thadd's voice.

He opened his eyes. His captain's features were an impassive mask.

"What?" Rhain asked.

"She asked where the Badus Mountains were." Thadd looked like he'd tasted something tart and unpleasant. "They said she didn't appear to know what the Barrens or the Radiance were."

Rhain frowned. "You think she's telling the truth? That she's not sent by my father?" Rhain was starting to suspect as much, but he wasn't sure he could trust his judgment where this woman was concerned.

Thadd spread his callused hands. "I don't know, but I'm not willing to take the risk."

Rhain felt a ping in the field.

Got you.

He spun and strode down the terrace. He moved close to one of the waterfalls arcing out into the lake below, elegant and beautiful.

He spotted her.

She stood on one of the railings, running along it with an inborn grace that was breathtaking. His gut clenched. If she fell...

He sprinted after her. "Mal!"

She teetered and looked back.

Then she sat on the railing and disappeared over the side.

Behind him, he heard Thadd curse.

Rhain reached the railing and looked over. Mal was climbing down toward the lower terrace.

"Mal, you can't get away."

She looked up. "I'm not your enemy, Rhain. I won't abandon my friend. I have to find her."

He ground his teeth together. She was loyal, but stubborn. *Gorr*, he admired her for it. "Stop. I'll help you find her."

Mal shot him a suspicious look. "We both know that if I come back up there, you'll lock me up again. I can't do it."

Rhain threw a leg over the railing. Thadd grabbed his arm.

"What in the *gorr* are you doing?"

"Going after her."

"No. If you fall—"

"It'll take us too long to get to the lower terrace. She'll be long gone."

A flyer flew over and the wash of air sprayed water from the waterfall on them.

Rhain gripped the railing. "I'm going after her."

"*Rhain*," Thadd growled.

"I'm not letting her get away."

"Why?"

Rhain paused. He couldn't really explain. He couldn't explain the strange compulsion in his gut.

He just knew he wasn't letting her escape him.

He started down the wall.

She saw him and sped up. The rock was wet from the spray from the waterfall. Rhain's fingers slipped.

"Mal, be careful, it's—"

She cried out.

He looked down...to see her falling.

No!

She waved her arms and legs, falling fast. Rhain threw a hand out, energy spearing from him, but she was already out of reach.

"Mal!"

She fell until she hit the water far, far below with a splash. It was a long fall. She could be hurt.

"I'll call for the water patrol," Thadd said. "They'll find her."

If she was still alive. If she was injured, she could drown before help reached her. Cursing, Rhain climbed back up, his gut churning. "I'm going down there—"

"Overlord!"

Two palace guards sprinted toward Rhain. He hauled himself over the railing and stood. "Yes?"

"A massive pack of hexids is moving through the countryside, headed this way."

Rhain froze. *What?* They never came this close to Citadel or the larger towns and cities. They darted in from the edges of the Barrens, but not into the heart of his territory.

"They wouldn't dare attack the city," Thadd said.

One of the guards shook her head. "They appear to be heading toward the town of Payeton."

A small town on the road into Citadel. It was a market town that specialized in selling flowers.

Its people were not warriors.

They'd be decimated.

"We have to get to Payeton," Thadd said.

Rhain's mouth firmed into a line, and he looked down at the water below. His hand curled into a fist.

"Rhain?" Thadd prompted.

"Thadd, organize the water patrol, and then let's get to Payeton."

He had a duty to his people. No one else was dying today. He'd see to them first, and then find Mallory.

Be alive, Mal West.

THE WATER WASHED over her head.

Mal came up spluttering. The lake seemed placid, but there were strong currents underneath.

The undertow pulled her along and she didn't fight it.

She looked up at the huge stone cliffs and terraces

towering above her. She noted that she was being pulled toward the adjacent rock wall.

When she spun around in the water, she spotted a large, round drain opening in the rock.

Oh, shit.

Mal tried to grab the edge of the drain, but it was no use. She was sucked into the tunnel.

Then the ride got wild.

The water picked up speed, racing faster through the tunnel. Soon she was in pitch blackness, and she got a few mouthfuls of water and spluttered. Every now and then, she could see glowing moss on the walls, outlining the circular form of the tunnel. She was spun around and around, and she tried desperately to keep her head above water. She kicked and spluttered.

She had no idea how long the roller-coaster went on for, but then she spotted a glimmer of light ahead.

Finally.

Suddenly, she was shot out over a short waterfall.

Hell.

She dropped, then hit a small pool of water with a giant splash.

The water pulled her gently along, then dumped her on a flat, grassy bank.

Ugh. She crawled out and spat the water out. She pushed to her knees and shoved her sodden hair back.

It could've been worse.

She looked up at the beautiful peaks that formed the ring of Citadel. A giant bridge arched overhead, leading into the heavily fortified main gate.

At least she was out of the city.

Mal sat for a moment, drawing her knees up to her chest. Right there, right now, she felt so goddamn alone. Her chest felt heavy, like it was filled with concrete.

She had no idea if Poppy was alive. She was on an alien planet being hunted by a man who thought she was an enemy spy.

She gave herself a minute to wallow. She'd find the strength to get up and keep going, but for a second, she just sat there and missed her mom, Rusty, and Poppy. The only people who'd ever given a shit about her.

Falling is a part of the process, Mal. It's how you dust yourself off and get back in the saddle that counts most.

"Thanks, Rusty," she muttered. "I'm not sure your cowboy-stunt man sayings apply on an alien world."

Finally, she pushed to her feet and wrung out her hair. Her clothes would dry in the sun. At least it wasn't cold.

She checked her sword and knife, then lifted her chin, and headed off into the trees.

They weren't too different from Earth, except every now and then, she passed some with red trunks and silver leaves. The dappled light flickered over her, and there were fresh, green smells. It was different than Earth, but still similar. An ache filled her.

The thought flashed into her mind that she might never see Earth again.

Okay, enough with the pity party, Mal.

A strange bird flittered onto a nearby branch. Its feathers glittered with a metallic sheen. It tweeted at her.

She hadn't gone far when she heard voices, a shout,

then the laughter of kids. She hesitated, then crept quietly forward. She pushed back the branches.

She was standing at the edge of a small town. Ahead, she saw neat, smooth streets. A transport, slick and quiet, zipped past, humming with energy. There were restaurants that circled around a pretty square, with a statue in the center.

Straightening, she wandered in, trying to act like she belonged.

She saw two men arguing, a projection up between them. Looked like a business deal gone bad. Most of the stalls sold flowers. Lush scents filled the air. What was it with flowers on Zhalto?

She glanced away and looked up to the sun. It was lower in the sky, so she knew which way was west. She swiveled and looked to the east. She needed some food and water so she could set out to find Poppy.

Mal chewed on her lip. She wasn't sure if she should go now. Night would fall soon, and she'd need shelter.

She scratched her arm. Thankfully, the itchiness wasn't as bad as it had been earlier.

She wandered the streets. The Zhaltons all looked happy and prosperous. She guessed his Overlordness wasn't a bad, tyrannical king.

Two flyers zipped overhead, and she watched them. They were going fast, moving away from Citadel.

She really needed to put some distance between her and the palace. Something warned her that Rhain was a man used to getting his own way.

She glanced up and realized she was close to the statue. She instantly recognized the rugged planes of the face. Rhain. He stood with those two jagged kilwar swords in hand, and even carved from stone, he looked powerful.

Mal felt a tug on her leg. She looked down and saw a cute kid, maybe two or three to her untrained eye, looking at her with huge gray eyes ringed with blue.

"Hey there." She looked around for the kid's mother or father. The boy held up a soggy-looking cracker. "Um, you have it. Thanks."

The kid munched on it.

Suddenly, shouts and screams echoed through the square.

Mal spun, her pulse kicking into gear. People were running down the street, staggering and almost tripping over.

Then she saw them.

The creatures were the same as the ugly one she'd fought at the crash site and in the dream with Rhain.

Hexids.

A pack of the damn monsters were loping toward the center of the town.

Shit. Fuck. Crap.

One attacked a woman, biting her arm and dragging her to the ground. Another one grabbed a man and tossed him into the air.

Mal reached over her shoulder and drew her sword, then looked down at the kid. He was wide-eyed, his mouth open.

"Uh-oh," the kid said.

Apparently that was universal.

Shit. Mal snatched him up. Still no sign of his

parents. She raced to the closest flower stall and pushed the boy up on the roof of the stall.

"Stay there, kid. I'll be back."

The boy nodded. "Back."

Mal turned. Some men armed with weapons raced toward the hexids.

Other people stood frozen.

"Get inside!" Mal yelled. "Lock the doors. Barricade them."

Turning, she stalked toward the hexids. She watched a man go down in a spray of blood.

Mal circled her sword, warming up her wrist.

She dragged in a deep, calming breath.

The lead beast locked its black eyes on her.

Bring it.

It bounded toward her. Mal lunged into the fight. She slashed out with a sword, catching the creature on its face.

It snarled, shaking its head and sidestepping.

She whirled and ran her sword down its ugly body, seeing its organs under that pale-gray skin.

Blood spilled, thick and black. The stench of rot and decay was overwhelming.

The creature staggered and fell, and she slashed her sword down, cutting deep into its neck.

She turned and saw a hexid take a screaming man down. She ran three steps and attacked, swinging her sword—left, right, left. Blood spurted. The hexid collapsed.

"Up." She yanked the man off the road.

"Thank you," he stammered.

The heat of the battle hit her. She narrowed in on her enemy, her prey.

She'd felt the same sensation when she'd flown into battle. She hadn't realized that some part of her had missed it.

With a roar, she attacked the next hexid. Skin split, more horrid blood spilled on the stone.

Her sword was a thing of pure beauty. As she swung it felt lighter and moved with ease. And it was sharper than anything she'd used before.

Several other men and a couple of women were fighting as well. Soon, Mal was splattered with blood and gore.

Then she heard a child's frightened scream.

No. She swiveled.

A hexid was menacing her boy. He clung to the roof of the stall, bawling. The hexid gathered its powerful muscles, readying to jump.

Oh no, you don't.

With a burst of speed, she ran. She felt a swell of energy and leaped, farther than she ever had before.

Mal lifted the sword over her head and brought it down hard, biting into the hexid's back.

With a vicious yowl, it spun and she tore into it with wild slashes and stabs. She lost herself in the fight. She had to protect the kid.

Finally, she got a clear shot and sank the blade deep into the hexid's gut.

The creature made a tortured sound, and she watched the light seep out of its black eyes.

She yanked her sword back.

"You're okay, kid." She snatched him down off the roof. She set him on her hip, and she saw big tears roll down his face.

"Bastin!" A woman ran over. "By the blooms. Thank you."

"*Mama*." The boy lurched for the woman.

He was safe. Mal released a breath and watched the woman hug the boy. She nodded at Mal, then ran for the buildings. Little Bastin waved at Mal over her shoulder.

She waved back.

Then she heard several growls.

Slowly, she turned, her fingers flexing on the hilt of her sword.

Two huge hexids slunk out of the shadows of the building, hunched over and claws flexing. A third creature was with them. It moved on four legs, had an armored, reptilian hide, and a long jaw with lots of teeth. It made her think of some prehistoric crocodile.

Great.

She lifted her sword.

The beasts rushed her.

Mal swung her sword, backing up.

A hexid leaped at her, claws slashing. She dodged to the side and felt the burn as they raked against her.

Goddammit.

The reptilian thing advanced. She saw implants embedded on its neck. Its jaws opened. The hexids closed in.

She couldn't fight all three at once, but she'd go down fighting.

She'd never thought that she would die alone on some distant alien world.

Then she heard a strange buzzing noise and a shadow crossed overhead.

She looked up and saw a flyer.

Suddenly, a body dropped from the ship.

A large muscular man landed in front of her with a bend of his powerful legs.

Mal felt the wash of energy over her, like a wave.

The creatures backed up, snarling.

Rhain straightened and glanced at her, his silver eyes shining. Then he reached over his shoulders and pulled out his two lethal blades.

The swords lit up, glowing red.

CHAPTER SEVEN

Rhain's blades were a blur as he hacked at the hexids.

Around him, Thadd and the rest of his elite guard dropped from the flyer above. They all drew their weapons—which lit up with different colors from orange to brilliant gold—and attacked.

A flash of movement at his side. He saw Mal tear into a hexid, swinging her sword. Helping him.

She was coated in dark blood, and he couldn't tell if she was hurt, or if any of the blood was hers.

If she was injured, it wasn't slowing her down. Her sword whirled, and she cut the hexid open.

The woman could fight. He'd watched her rescue the child.

A terrified scream cut through the fight.

Both he and Mal turned, just in time to see a hexid drag a screaming young woman around a building.

Gorr.

Mal took off. Rhain ran one step behind her.

They sprinted around the building. The hexid was dragging the struggling woman into the trees.

Rhain gritted his teeth. His *gorr*-taken father had gone too far. Rhain would never forgive him for killing innocent Zhaltons as part of his sick game.

Mal raced ahead, and they sprinted into the forest.

"Which way?" She scanned around. There was no sign of the beast, but Rhain sensed it not far away.

"This way." He pushed through the undergrowth.

The birds and creatures had gone silent.

They reached a small clearing that was covered in blooming white flowers like a patterned rug.

Some were crushed.

"Here." Mal lifted her sword and followed the trail.

They moved through the trees and a small animal—a cute, fluffy ixia—cut past them.

A woman's scream filled the air.

They swiveled. Mal looked at him and they nodded.

Thadd would be mad that Rhain had run off without him, but he needed to save the woman. He wouldn't let another Zhalton die.

He and Mal broke out of the trees. They were near the river, the cliffs of Citadel looming overhead.

Mal crouched. "Blood." She touched her fingertips together.

"They're close. Somewhere toward the rock face."

They moved closer and Rhain saw the mouth of the cave in the cliff wall. The mountains were riddled with natural caves and tunnels.

"I feel the hexid." He spun his blades.

Suddenly, the hexid leaped onto a large, flat rock in

front of them, holding the squirming, terrified woman in its claws.

It released her and she tumbled down the rocks with a scream.

"Here!" Mal waved at the woman.

Rhain leaped at the hexid. He slashed and stabbed.

Out of the corner of his eye, he saw the wild-eyed woman stagger toward Mal.

"Go," Mal yelled. "Get back to town."

The woman sobbed, then nodded and ran off, limping, into the trees.

Rhain thrust his blade deep, but hit bone. Mal jumped up beside him and cut fast, her sword moving in a blur.

"Charge your sword," he said.

"I don't know how." She sliced again.

"Pull on the energy field, and direct it to your sword."

"I thought you said only Zhaltons could do that?"

True, but he'd sensed her use some energy before, when they were in the medica ward. Maybe she had some latent Zhalton genes?

"Try it."

The hexid leaped away, bleeding badly.

"I can't do it." She lifted her sword, staring at it. Suddenly, it started to glow with a silver-white light. "Holy hell."

Rhain sucked in a breath. No Zhalton could charge silver-white. Red was the highest energy level.

The silver glow intensified.

"Use it!" he said.

She leaped off the rock. The hexid snarled and

reared, and Mal attacked it. With a wild slash, she sliced its throat. Her charged sword moved faster, the sharp edge cutting deeper.

The beast collapsed.

Chest heaving, Mal stepped back, staring at her sword with shock.

"How is this even possible? I can...feel the energy."

Then Rhain heard the crunch of a twig.

They both spun.

Six hexids slunk out of the cave mouth.

Rhain cursed.

"We've been had," Mal muttered. "They lured us out here to attack you."

Six would be tough, even for the two of them. "There are too many."

One darted forward, aiming for Rhain. Mal leaped in front of him and drove her sword into the hexid's eye. Its jaws snapped, a whisper from her face, but she didn't even flinch.

He cursed and stabbed it, twisting his blades.

It collapsed.

But the others were moving in.

"Can we outrun them?" she asked.

"No."

She scanned around. "Can they climb trees?"

"No, but they can jump. And they can bring trees down."

"Great. Wait." She pointed. "Can they climb walls?"

Rhain saw the ledge high above the cave mouth.

He narrowed his gaze. "That might work. Let's get up there. My guards will find us eventually."

"Okay, so we get past them, climb—"

"I have a better idea." He shoved his swords in their sheaths, then wrapped an arm around her and lifted her off her feet.

"Hey, what are you doing?"

"I can jump up there."

Her eyes widened. "That high? While holding me?" Her hand flexed on his shoulder.

"Yes."

Rhain pulled the energy in, then jumped up—

A huge pain burned up his leg and they were wrenched wildly downward.

Gorr. A hexid was clamped onto his boot and he felt the prick of the fangs in his calf.

They crashed to the ground.

"I hate hexids." Mal rolled to her feet.

Rhain held his palm up. The pulse of energy he released hit the hexid and the animal reared back.

Then it snarled, its muscles bunching, ready to attack.

Rhain wouldn't have time to get his swords out.

Mal leaped between him and the hexid, pulling her blade impossibly fast.

She and the creature collided.

The blade disappeared into the creature's chest, but he saw it slash at her.

"Mal!" Blocking the pain in his leg, he lunged for her.

She fell back into his arms, her stomach bleeding. Her sword pulled free of the dying hexid.

Without waiting, Rhain leaped into the air, using all his power to drive high.

They sailed through the air and landed on the rock ledge.

"You little idiot." He dropped down, holding her in his lap.

"Saved you." She gasped out, pressing her hand to the gashes on her stomach. Blood oozed between her fingers.

"Quiet." She'd saved him. She'd risked her life for his.

She didn't belong to his father. Rhain knew that in his gut.

He had to stop the bleeding, or she'd die before anyone found them. His brows drew together. His energy wasn't attuned to healing, so it didn't come easily to him, and he wasn't good at it.

But he had to try.

He lifted her blood-stained palm off her belly, then moved his own over it. She moaned.

"*Shh.* I need to stop the bleeding." He felt the energy coalesce inside him, whipping around. It wanted a target to kill, not to heal. He ground his teeth together, red energy curling around his hand, then he directed it into the wound.

"Hurts," she hissed.

"Sorry." He felt her watching him.

"This...isn't easy for you," she said.

"My energy skills are not the best fit for healing."

"Zhaltons can all use energy?"

He realized she was trying to distract herself from the pain. He felt his own discomfort grow as his energy tried to heal her. "To varying degrees. Some can only feel it, and not utilize it for much. Others are very strong. Some can heal, some can kill, and others use it with technology, to power equipment. We've found ways to harness it to power our vehicles."

"Your pretty flyers." She huffed out a breath. "The blue energy."

He nodded. "Blue is the lowest energy level. Healers' energy is green. Then orange, gold, and red are increasing levels of power."

"Yours is red." She looked at the glow on his palm.

"Yes, only the Zhalton royal family has red energy." And hers was a brilliant silver-white. Where was she from? *What* was she?

"You charged your weapon, Mal."

"I...don't know how I did it. I'm not Zhalton—" She groaned in pain.

Rhain fought back a curse. "I'm sorry, Mal. I know it hurts."

But he saw her injury improving a little. The bleeding had slowed.

"I...can handle it." Her body arched a little. "*Fuck.*"

Rhain stilled. He'd heard that strange word before. On Carthago.

His energy cut off.

He met her pain-filled gaze. "Rhain?"

"You're from Earth," he said.

Her eyes widened, then her face went pale, and she lost consciousness.

MAL WOKE TO THE NOW-FAMILIAR, white, octagonal-tiled ceiling.

"We meet again."

Tavith came into view.

Mal pressed a hand to her stomach. She felt a faint twinge, but there were no bloody wounds.

"Don't worry, I healed you all up." The medica scowled. "Are you going to make a habit of running into danger and getting hurt?"

"Probably."

He sighed. "Well, I guess you'll keep me busy."

"What happened?" She sat up. "Why am I alive?"

"Our illustrious overlord carried you in here, growling at us to fix you."

Hmm.

"He said you threw yourself in front of a hexid. Actually, quite a few of them."

"It seemed like the right thing to do."

Tavith's eyes narrowed, but he remained silent.

Her memories were a little murky. "He's okay?"

The medica nodded. "I healed his leg." Tavith waved a hand at the empty chair beside her bed. "He then proceeded to sleep in that chair and watch over you all night. Which meant his captain of the guard also stayed, leaning against the wall and glowering. Our stubborn overlord only left when some of his advisors dragged him out of here to deal with some pressing issues."

Mal remembered something. Her chest hitched.

Rhain had mentioned Earth.

She looked out the window and saw it was evening. The huge moon was visible on the horizon and... Wow, more pretty auroras. The sky was full of color. "I slept all night and all day?"

"Yes. One thing our overlord is *not* good at is healing. I had to re-do some of his work. Don't get me wrong, he saved your life by stopping the blood gushing out of you."

Mal winced. "I couldn't let his Overlordness get eaten."

"But by the time I'd finished with you, your body needed rest. Added to that, the scans I've done on your body show...some changes."

"Changes?" That didn't sound good.

"Your body is reacting to our Zhalton environment."

Mal scraped a hand through her hair. "The magnetic field?"

The medica nodded.

"What does that mean? That I'll...develop some Zhalton abilities?" That already appeared to be happening. "Or I'll get sick and die?"

"I honestly don't know. You don't seem to be getting weaker, and Rhain mentioned you wielded energy in the fight."

She gave the man a clipped nod.

"I'll continue to monitor you." Tavith spread his hands wide. "That's all I can tell you right now."

Her thoughts turned to Poppy. She was out there, somewhere, alone for yet another day. Mal swallowed her worry.

She realized that she wasn't tied to the bed this time. "No handcuffs. This is new."

Tavith nodded.

Mal slipped off the bed. She realized her skin and hair were clean, and she was wearing a new set of bra and panties. Tavith held up some pants and a nice halter top in an emerald-green color.

She dressed in them and wandered to the window.

Jeez. Light filled the night sky, like a multicolored river. The auroras were gorgeous.

"You have an invitation," Tavith said.

She raised a brow.

"Overlord Sarkany has invited you to dine with him."

Her gaze narrowed. "Is that a polite way to say interrogation?"

"No. But I don't believe you have a choice."

She sighed. "Right. Where?"

Tavith swiveled and a brawny man stepped forward.

He was tall and muscled, with short hair and a jaw that looked made of stone. His eyes were a brilliant, sapphire blue. She'd seen him fighting the hexids.

He scowled at her.

"This is the overlord's captain of the guard, Thadd Naveri. He will show you the way."

Thadd's heavy scowl said the man would prefer to escort her over the side of a cliff.

"All right. Thanks again, Tavith."

"Try not to get killed. Or take on another pack of hexids."

"Or fall into the lake," Thadd added.

Clearly, he'd seen her fall.

Tavith blinked. "You fell in the lake?"

Mal winked. "I kind of jumped."

"You did not," Thadd said.

"Okay, lead on, Mr. Dark and Scowly."

Impossibly, the man's scowl deepened. He led her out of the medica ward and down the corridor.

"Mal," she said.

"Thadd. If you pose a risk to the overlord, I will kill you."

"Got it. As I've mentioned, I've no desire to kill your overlord, and I don't work for your enemy. I just want to find my friend."

They moved up some steps. People eyed her, curiosity on their faces. He led her up another set of steps. At the top, Thadd pushed open a heavy door. It opened onto a rooftop terrace.

He nodded and closed the door behind her.

The auroras stole her breath. There were mostly blues and greens, changing to pink toward the horizon.

She arched her head back and breathed deeply. The tension she hadn't realized she was holding eased.

"You like the auroras."

The deep voice made her jump. She hadn't heard him. Rhain stepped up beside her.

"We get auroras on our planet too. But not like this, and just occasionally at the poles when the conditions are right."

"You're from Earth."

She turned to face him. His face was shadowed, which of course just made him more masculine and intriguing.

"I am. How do you know?"

"I've met some people from your planet."

Mal sucked in a breath, realizing what that meant. "The human survivors on Carthago."

Rhain inclined his head.

Mal's heart thudded, beating like a drum in her ears. "Is Carthago close?"

"It isn't far."

Oh, God. "That means we aren't close to Earth."

"No. I'm sorry, Mal. From what Imperator Galen told me—he's the man who gave those from Earth sanctuary—your planet is on the other side of the galaxy. It would take several lifetimes to reach it with our fastest ships."

She staggered. She caught herself, but felt a crushing sense of aloneness close in.

She'd never grab a beer with her fellow pilots at the bar, she'd never see her Breitling watch or Rusty's sword collection again, and she'd never play the battered guitar she secretly loved. Rusty had given it to her for her birthday when she was nine. Hell, she'd never eat peanuts again.

A hand touched her back. "Mal. Breathe." There was a snap of authority in his voice.

She swallowed and sucked in air. He led her to a couch and she dropped onto it heavily. It was soft, and dipped as he sat down beside her.

"How did you get here?" he asked.

"We were testing a new method of space travel. Based on information sent from the Carthago survivors. Something went wrong."

He reached over and poured a drink. She realized the low table in front of them was laden with food.

"We opened up a wormhole. We were just supposed to travel within our solar system, not get flung to the other side of the galaxy."

He handed her a glass.

Mal sipped, barely tasting the sweet juice. She put the drink back down on the table.

Once again, she didn't belong. Her life had just been a series of places she'd never fit. Her biological father hadn't stuck around to even see her born. She'd been terrified when her mother had died, but being with Rusty was the closest thing she'd had to a home. Looking back, she could see it wasn't the ideal life for a young girl, but she'd been happy.

She'd been sure she'd found her place in the Air Force, but it hadn't taken long to see she was a square peg in a round hole. She doubted she would have lasted long at Nynatech.

Now, she was lost on an alien planet with nothing, and if she didn't find Poppy, no one.

"You have sanctuary here, Mal."

She met those fascinating silver eyes. "I thought I was a suspected enemy agent."

"You may have been at first, but not now. One, you're from Earth. Two, it's clear that Zhalto is unfamiliar to you, and three, you stupidly risked your life to save mine."

She snorted. "You're welcome."

"You almost died. Your wounds required hours of healing. *Never* put yourself between me and a predator again."

She leaned in, anger flaring. She latched onto it. It was much better than the fear, sorrow, grief, and knowing she had no way home.

"Oh, I won't. You know what? Next time, I might *push* you at the damn hexid."

Rhain snorted.

"You're an arrogant ass," she snapped.

He caught her chin, and she clamped her hand on his thick wrist.

"Don't touch me, or I'll take you down," she said.

"You could try, but I highly doubt you'd succeed."

She narrowed her gaze. "I could totally take you."

"You must still be injured. You appear to have delusions."

They shifted closer, until their bodies brushed.

His fingers tightened on her chin.

The air lodged in her lungs. He smelled so damn good. He was solid, warm, and real in all the craziness. "*Rhain...*"

He lowered his head.

Mal made a sound, and slid her hands into his thick hair, dragged his mouth to hers.

Holy cow.

The kiss was bold, sensuous, and hot. He didn't waste time being tentative, nor did she. She tangled her tongue with his, drawing in his taste. He growled and she enjoyed the pure pleasure that spiraled through her.

His hand untied her hair and it spilled around her shoulders. He stroked it through his fingers.

"It's so soft," he murmured against her lips.

"Don't stop," she whispered.

Mal didn't want to think. She wanted to stay lost in this pleasure.

He kissed her again and her panties went damp. His

mouth moved across her cheekbone, and she realized he was kissing her small beauty spot on her cheek. His finger stroked her eyebrow.

"How did you get this scar?"

"Bar fight." She'd been fourteen. She and Rusty had been grabbing a burger, and a fight had broken out. She hadn't ducked quick enough.

She dragged Rhain's mouth back to hers.

One of his hands cupped her breast, and she pushed into that touch. He made a sound, part growl, part groan. As he toyed with her nipple, she moved her mouth along his firm jaw, then nipped it.

God, she was so lost in the pleasure, she couldn't think straight. Nothing else mattered, only Rhain, only this heat between them.

The sound of a door opening had her springing back from him. They were both breathing heavily.

Rhain growled.

Two servers in long tunics stepped inside. "Is there anything you require from the kitchens, my lord?" one asked.

"No."

With quick nods, the man and woman backed out.

Mal rose, her movements jerky. Her head cleared a little now. Enough that she could think.

When Rhain was close, all she could think about was him. And getting her hands on him. And what he'd look like naked.

She gripped the back of her neck. She had no business thinking about getting laid when Poppy was out there, alone, scared.

"I... Well..." She scraped a hand over her face. "Shit."

He cleared his throat, and she noticed the flush along his cheekbones. "Mal—"

She threw an arm into the air. "Did you use some sort of energy magic on me?"

His face darkened. "No."

"There is only one thing I want. One thing I have to focus on, and that's finding my friend."

He was silent.

She cleared her throat. "This...can't happen. I'm so far from home, can never return—" her voice cracked and she hated it "—and Tavith said I'm changing. That Zhalto is altering me somehow." She shook her head. "I only have the bandwidth to deal with finding Poppy."

His face shut down and he took a step back.

Mal's heart squeezed, suddenly hating the distance between them. God, she was confused.

"I don't make a habit of taking advantage of vulnerable women."

She bristled. "I'm not vulnerable."

"Like you said, you're dealing with a lot."

"I need to go—"

His head whipped up. "You wouldn't survive a day in the Barrens."

She gritted her teeth. "I have to—"

He held up a hand. "You're a formidable fighter, Mal, but the Barrens combined with Krastin and his beasts... that's something you can't take on alone."

She sagged. "I *have* to find Poppy."

Rhain watched her steadily, then he nodded. "I'll help you."

CHAPTER EIGHT

The next morning, Mal paced the corridor with its shiny, polished floor and pots of blooming flowers.

The night before, Rhain had left her at the door of a plush bedroom, with a promise to collect her today.

And a promise to look for Poppy.

Mal had slept well, but she'd had weird dreams.

She dreamed of being pulled in a certain direction, like a compulsion. She rubbed the center of her chest. It ached.

Her other dreams were of kissing Rhain.

And doing a lot more than kissing.

God. She sagged against the wall. She'd kissed an alien king.

She shook her head. It had been a hell of a kiss, but right now, she was shoving it away in her mental "crazy shit to deal with later" box.

Some women walked past her—beautiful, elegant, soft-looking—covered in perfume scents, with flowers in their hair. They eyed her curiously.

Mal was pretty sure her leather pants and fitted, black top weren't up to scratch. She was wearing fresh clothes that had been left for her. Like magic, they were the perfect size. She'd had a glorious, extra-long shower both last night and this morning. The fancy shower had water, but also some ray of yellow light. She felt cleaner than she ever had before. She looked at her callused hands. She wasn't—and never would be—beautiful, elegant or soft, and she didn't want to be. She could clean up and managed fit and pretty. That was enough for her.

Heavy footsteps sounded.

She looked up and saw Rhain heading in her direction.

The impact of him hit her. Damn, the guy was really something. That irresistible blend of masculine attraction and power. He wore a fitted, black, sleeveless shirt tucked into his leather pants. A large belt circled his lean hips and red fabric was tucked around it. The hilts of his swords were visible over his shoulders.

The women in the flirty dresses curtsied, interested looks on their faces. Rhain nodded at them.

Mal's nose wrinkled. He probably had a harem of gorgeous women to do his every bidding.

That silver gaze swept over her. "Good morning, Mal."

"Your Overlordness." She did a bad impression of the women's curtsies.

His gaze narrowed. "When my people do that, I sense respect. When you do it, I sense the opposite."

"Guess I did it right, then."

He shook his head, like he didn't quite know what to make of her. "Are you ready?"

She nodded. Her sword rested on her back, safe in its scabbard.

"Did you pay the weapons shop?" She'd asked him to pay for the sword and knife she'd stolen.

"I did. They overlooked your theft because they were ecstatic to get a recommendation from the overlord."

They walked side-by-side down the hall.

"When do we leave?" she asked.

"I know you are eager to find Poppy, but we need to plan, first."

He led her into a large room with huge windows that flooded the place with light.

Grumpy Thadd was there. She traded a hard stare with the man. She wondered if he ever smiled. There were two other guards—one male and one female. The man had long brown hair in a braid, was slender, but all muscle. He'd be fast. He had multiple daggers in a harness across his chest.

The woman had short, blonde hair and held herself tall, her hand on the hilt of the sword at her hip. Swordswoman.

"Mal West, I believe you met my captain of the guard, Thadd, and these are two of my elite fighters, Trist and Carvia."

"Hi." Mal lifted a hand.

Rhain moved to the large, circular table that dominated the space. He waved a hand and a 3-D projection of rough terrain appeared on the surface.

"We've triangulated where the other large piece of

your ship fell." He swiped the projection and then zoomed in.

"This is your crash site." Thadd pointed to a glowing, gold mark. "And this is the other crash site."

It was a red dot, near a mountainous area.

"The Badus Mountains," Rhain said.

"Horrid place," Carvia murmured.

The projection zoomed in, and images appeared.

Mal sucked in a breath. They showed dark rock and pools of lava. She watched as a geyser shot molten rock into the air.

"It's very dangerous," Rhain said. "Millennia ago, our system was hit by the Radiance."

She nodded. "A huge solar flare."

"Yes. Massive radiation cascaded through the Sarkany System. Andret, the planet closest to the sun, had its atmosphere burned away. The advanced species that lived there was killed. The planet is now a lump of rock. Here on Zhalto, the composition of the core of our planet strengthened the magnetic field."

"It offered you more protection."

He nodded. "It didn't stop the Radiance, but yes, it offered some protection."

Mal pressed her hands to the table. "Some still got through."

"Yes, the worst of it was what caused the Barrens. It irradiated animals, killed millions of Zhaltons. The animals left behind mutated into wild beasts. Zhaltons on the rest of the planet were also affected by the flare. They were changed. We gained the ability to manipulate energy from our magnetic field."

"So the Barrens is a tough landscape filled with monsters."

"Right. Getting to the crash site has an added complication." An image appeared in the projection.

The man wasn't tall, maybe a few inches taller than her, and lean. He held himself ramrod straight. His head was shaved, except for a black strip of hair down the center of his head.

"This is Krastin. The one directing the hexids and coordinating the attacks on my people." A muscle ticked in Rhain's jaw. "He's made a base in the Barrens, near the Badus Mountains somewhere."

Mal pulled a face. "So, to find Poppy, we have to head right into the heart of Krastin's base."

"Yes."

God. Her chest was tight. Was there any way Poppy could have survived? Could she have survived the crash, and the Barrens?

Mal had to find out. She had to at least try. It wasn't in her nature to give up and just stay safe.

"So, what's the plan?"

"We work together. We check out the second crash site, and pinpoint Krastin's base."

Ah, so he didn't really want to find Poppy. "You need to find him."

"I want to crush him." Rhain's tone darkened. "Make him pay for killing my people."

His tone made her shiver. *All right.* "When do we leave?"

Thadd straightened. "We are readying a flyer now. We'll fly in, straight over the crash site. Several fighters will come with us."

"Let's go," she said.

Soon, Mal found herself on a huge landing pad on the upper level of the palace. She was wearing metallic armor on her torso—thanks to Carvia. It was made of a flexible metal that was surprisingly comfortable.

She had a birds-eye view of Citadel. It really was beautiful.

She turned to look at the flyer.

It was beautiful, as well. It spoke to her pilot's heart. She saw two pilots in sleek flight suits circling the flyer, doing the Zhalton equivalent of pre-flight checks.

"Ready?"

She turned to Rhain. She hadn't heard him, but she'd sensed him. *Crap.* Tavith was right. She was changing and becoming more sensitive to the planet's energy field.

He was in his armor—a dark bronze, with that interesting medallion set in the center of it.

"I'm ready."

"Then let's go." He waved her aboard the flyer.

Inside was plush and comfortable. Curved seats filled the main cabin. The two pilots settled in seats in the cockpit, readying for take-off.

Hard-edged fighters followed them in. Trist leaped aboard, his long braid whipping behind his trim body. He smiled at her. Carvia followed and nodded. They all carried different weapons—ones that they could charge with energy.

Mal needed to practice more with that. She could bury her head in the sand about her growing abilities, or embrace them. She sighed. Rusty had another saying about that. *If you go through life with your head in the sand, then all people will see is your ass.*

"Prepare for take-off," a pilot called back.

Mal leaned forward eagerly, watching the pilots manipulating the controls. She saw a blue glow from the cockpit screens and from the pilots' hands.

"They use energy to control the ship?" she asked.

Rhain nodded. "Some Zhaltons are attuned to machines. The energy interface lets them control all parts of the ship quickly and seamlessly."

Energy flared, raising the hairs on her arms.

The flyer lifted off and flew out over the lake.

Wow. Mal pressed close to the window. Citadel flashed past below them.

Then they were soaring out over the mountainous ring that formed the city. Green fields spread out before them, dotted with flowers.

"You have so many flowers."

"One of our main crops here on Zhalto." He pointed past her, his body brushing hers.

And of course, every part of her took notice.

She looked at the farmland. "What do you do with them?"

"They've lots of uses. For beauty and medicines. Some are edible, some are rich in energy. We can harvest that energy as a power source. We export some to other planets and systems."

"That's incredible. Our flowers on Earth have far fewer uses."

He cocked his head. "Do you miss Earth?"

"It's home. What I know. My job was decent, and I

got to fly. I'll miss my favorite watch, and the sword collection my stepfather left me. There are a few you'd even like." She sighed. "I'll miss peanuts."

"Peanuts?"

"A nut we eat as a snack. I got addicted to them when I was flying in the military."

"I should have guessed you had military training."

"I was a pilot in my country's Air Force, but it wasn't long before they didn't want me."

Rhain raised a surprised brow.

"Apparently, I'm not very good at following orders."

He smiled, and her chest hitched. It turned the rugged to handsome. Her fingers curled into her palm.

"So, what are peanuts like?" he asked.

"A small nut. I like them roasted and salty."

"And what about people? Is there anyone grieving for you? A lover or partner?"

She swallowed. "No. I lost Rusty, my stepfather, a few months back." She clasped her hands together. "I have no family waiting for me, or anyone who'll miss me."

"I'm sorry." His hand closed over hers. "It's hard to lose someone you love."

She looked at him, saw something in his silver gaze. "You lost someone?"

"My mother. Over a decade ago."

"I'm sorry, Rhain. My mother died too, when I was eight."

He looked up. "She was murdered. Krastin killed her."

"*What*?" Mal breathed.

"My father ordered the assassination. She defied him

at every turn, and ensured I wanted nothing to do with him."

Mal rested her hand on his knee. "Rhain—"

"I want him dead, Mal."

The ruthless cut to his voice made her chest hitch. She saw a darkness on his face she hadn't seen before. It scared the hell out of her.

"Poppy's my priority," she said.

"And Krastin is mine."

Okay. Mal bit her lip. She needed to keep a sharp eye on this, because for Rhain, this mission was very, very personal.

Rhain straightened, then pointed out the window. "There's the Barrens in the distance."

She saw the darker smudge and the faint shadow of mountains.

I'm coming, Poppy.

THE BARRENS WERE dark and forbidding. Rhain, and the rulers before him, had tried over the years to rehabilitate it, but it was too irradiated and damaged.

It was part of Zhalto now. Bad to the good. Dark to the light.

Thankfully, the mutated monsters of the Barrens only came out at night.

He glanced over at Mal.

Her face was set, a little grim. Her fingers curled securely on a handhold.

He knew he'd unsettled her earlier. He flexed his

hand. The need to hunt down Krastin was growing stronger. He'd killed Rhain's people, murdered Rhain's mother, threatened Rhain's leadership, and he had to be stopped.

Rhain cursed mentally. He sounded too much like his father.

Blowing out a breath, he studied Mal. Such strength. She was so far from her home, her life changed irrevocably. Yet she was determined to find her friend. He'd already learned from his friends on Carthago that humans could be brave, loyal, and strong. Mal was living up to that description.

She turned her head and their gazes met. She was fierce. He knew she'd keep fighting, surviving, searching for Poppy.

"We'll fly over the crash site soon," he said.

She nodded.

"After that, we'll head to the Emex Mining Outpost. It's secure. A safe base for us to use while we search for Krastin."

"Got it," she replied.

"We'll find out what happened to your friend."

Mal shifted. "What if she's dead?"

Her tone was devoid of emotion, but he knew there was pain under it.

He touched Mal's arm. "Then we'll mourn her."

"I'll be alone," she whispered.

"No, you won't be."

She grabbed his hand and held on tight.

"And Carthago isn't far away. You can meet with the others from Earth."

Her eyes lit up. "I'd love to meet them."

"Coming up on the crash site coordinates," the lead pilot called out.

The ground below changed. The lava pools glowed brightly.

"It looks like hell," she murmured. "A mythical place where the damned are sent when they die."

In the distance, a geyser shot up, spraying hot lava into the air. Rhain felt the tension radiating from Mal. She tapped a boot on the floor.

"It's too dangerous to land," the pilot said.

"Get us as low as you can," Rhain ordered.

He rose and opened the side door of the flyer. The ship moved into a hover. Mal stepped up beside him.

It only took seconds to see the twisted remains of the ship.

She sucked in a sharp breath.

"Scan it," Rhain said.

A blue light shot out from the flyer, moving over the wreckage.

"No life signs, Overlord. And no significant biological matter."

"She's not here." Mal turned to him and pressed a hand to his chest. "She's not dead."

There was hope in her eyes and he didn't want to dash it. There was every chance some predator had dragged off Poppy's body.

Mal's fingers curled into him. "She might've made it, Rhain."

"She might have." But where would she have gone?

Even if she'd been alive, she would have had to face the Barrens.

A low alarm filled the flyer. The fighters all stiffened.

The two pilots were working frantically, looking at a projection.

"Status?" Rhain called out.

"Overlord. We have four starships incoming. Fast."

Rhain frowned. "From where?"

"No idea. They appeared out of nowhere. They're coming into scanning range." The older man looked back. "Sir, they're Zhylaw."

Thadd cursed.

Gorr. "Let's go. Evasive maneuvers."

"You won't fight them?" Mal asked.

"The flyer is a transport. It doesn't have the offensive capabilities to take on that many ships."

"Sir, they're in visual range."

Back at the side door, Rhain gripped the edge, looking out into the sky. He saw the black ships streaking closer.

They had sharp pointed fronts, extending back to a jagged backend that looked almost like teeth—sharp and intimidating. Zhylaw raiders. They were fast and deadly.

The raiders fired.

The flyer dove. Rhain slammed into the wall and Mal crashed into him. He wrapped an arm around her.

Out the window, a raider zoomed past. The flyer dipped and weaved to evade.

"Those ships—" Mal's nose wrinkled.

"Yes, they have organic components built into them." Parts of the raiders were constructed of skin and bone.

She grimaced. "They harvest parts of living things to use in the ships?"

"Yes."

She shook her head.

"You'd better strap in," Thadd growled at them.

Rhain urged Mal into a seat. The flyer shuddered and he slammed into the wall, barely catching himself. He dropped into the seat beside Mal.

Smoke filled the cabin.

Gorr. They'd been hit.

Several raiders crossed in front of them. The pilot jerked the flyer to the side, banking hard.

Mal cursed and bumped against Rhain's shoulder.

"Surely I can't be in two ship crashes in one week," she muttered.

"It'll be fine. This flyer is sturdy."

But they took another hit, and the flyer jolted hard.

They started to spin in a circle, dizzyingly fast. There were mutters and shouts from the fighters, all of them gripping their seats.

Gorr. Rhain threw an arm around Mal.

"We're going down," the lead pilot yelled.

"Hold on." Rhain unclipped his harness.

"What are you doing?" Mal yelled.

"Saving us."

He staggered toward the cockpit. It was so hard to walk with the flyer jerking and shuddering.

He made it, and watched the ground rising to meet them through the front viewscreen. He lifted a palm, and pulled all the energy he could, as fast as he could. He needed to slow them down and buffer their landing or they'd be smashed to tiny pieces.

He gritted his teeth. He felt the energy gather. *Come on.*

The flyer slowed, but not enough.

They hit the ground with a jarring thump.

Rhain was tossed forward, then backward. He slammed to the floor, his head striking something hard.

He must've lost consciousness because the next thing he knew, hands were touching his face.

"Rhain? *Rhain.*"

Mal. He really liked the strong lines of her face. Interesting, attractive, and subtly different.

"Mal." He cupped her cheek.

Relief leaked into her green-gold eyes. "We made it, thanks to you."

Thadd appeared behind her. "You all right?"

Rhain nodded. "I'm fine." He pushed to his feet. The back of his head throbbed but his vision seemed fine.

Someone had opened the side door. Outside, he knew his fighters would have set up sentries.

"The Zhylaw?" Rhain asked.

"They flew away," Thadd said.

That wasn't good. "Reinforcements?"

"The pilots called for help. Ruggers are inbound, but it'll take them a while to reach us."

"Okay."

They disembarked from the ship. Once outside, Rhain stared at a lava pool nearby. Luckily, they hadn't crash-landed in it.

The pilots were studying the wreck of the flyer.

"Any chance it will fly?" Rhain asked.

The senior pilot shook his head. "The energy capacitor is damaged."

"All right. We'll wait for our rescue from the outpost, and defend ourselves until it arrives."

Mal scanned the empty landscape. "It doesn't look too bad."

"Overlord. To the east," a fighter called out.

Rhain and Mal swiveled.

She groaned. "I'm just the universe's punching bag, I swear."

It was a dust cloud.

They watched it, and a second later, Rhain squinted to make out what was generating it. A flood of creatures sprinted toward them.

They weren't hexids.

"I saw one of those reptilian things in town," Mal said.

"They're called *cupra*. Heavily armored, and with a very powerful bite. Another Zhylaw creation."

She drew her sword. "How do you take them down?"

"With great difficulty."

"Wonderful." She rotated her sword.

"Fighters, form up," Thadd bellowed, pulling his own sword from its sheath. A second later, it charged a brilliant gold. Nearby, Carvia hefted a beautiful saber that gleamed with an orange charge.

"Charge your weapon," Rhain said.

Mal screwed up her face, concentrating.

He touched her arm. "Relax. Don't fight it. We need to get you some training."

He felt a lick of power between them. She gasped. Deep in her eyes, he witnessed a faint glow of silver.

Her sword charged, glowing silver-white.

Rhain heard the gasps of shock from the other fighters.

"Ready?" he asked.

"Oh, yeah."

CHAPTER NINE

The creatures, the cupra, raced closer.

They really did look like fast-moving, mutant crocodiles.

Mal watched several fighters firing charged crossbows.

Boom.

Boom.

Boom.

The bolts hit, exploding on contact. Cupra parts flew into the air.

The rest kept coming.

In the distance, Mal spotted something. "Rhain!"

He followed her gaze.

It was some sort of ground transport. It was the same black color as the Zhylaw ships, with black spikes rising at the back of it. A lean man stood at the front.

Bald except for a strip of black hair down the middle of his skull.

Rhain sucked in a breath. "Krastin."

The man was watching impassively. Mal's grip tightened on her sword hilt. *Asshole.*

Rhain frowned. "There's someone with him."

Mal strained to see. "Where?"

"Kneeling—"

She caught the glint of blonde hair. Her heart contracted. She knew that slender body and hair. "It's Poppy!"

Mal took off running.

"Mal!" Rhain roared behind her.

The first cupra reached her. Powered by her rage, she swung her sword and slashed at it.

It opened its huge jaws.

Yes, yes, what big, meat-ripping teeth you have.

It snapped at her and she dodged to the side. Near the neck, she could see a faint change in the coloring where the dark scales didn't overlap as thickly. There was also the faint line of an implant in that area.

Hello, weak spot.

She spun, and ran in from the side and slashed again.

Her blade cut into that thin spot. Not like butter, she still had to push it, but it cut deep.

Blood splattered, filled with a rotten reek. The cupra made a screeching sound and snapped its jaws at her again.

Die, damn you. She had to get to Poppy.

She ran along the side of the creature. She spotted another weak spot in the scales and stabbed deep, puncturing something.

It roared.

Rhain leaped on its back. The deadly strike of his

dual swords was impressive. Energy pulsed off them, beheading the creature.

Mal heaved in a breath. There was no time to think; another cupra rushed at her.

She dropped low, under the fangs, and cut into the creature's legs with a brutal swing.

Mal charged on. Around her, Rhain's fighters had their weapons out, swinging, filling the air with punches of power.

She hacked into another cupra, and Rhain did as well.

She looked up and saw that the transport carrying Krastin and Poppy was moving away.

"No!" Mal cried.

A cupra leaped on her while she was preoccupied and took her to the ground. She felt the prick of claws, saw the jaws descending.

No, dammit. She wasn't dying here.

She rammed her sword up.

Power, like a ball of energy, exploded along her sword. The cupra tore apart and she was drenched in blood and... ugh, she didn't want to know.

Rhain yanked her up. "What was that?"

"No idea." The power had just flowed from her.

She looked up. The transport was headed into some rock formations.

"We can't let them get away."

Rhain's jaw tightened. "Thadd!"

The captain appeared, black blood decorating his chest in a diagonal spray. His sword dripped with it.

"Leave most of the fighters here to defend the flyer

and deal with the last of the cupra. Get two fighters. We're going after Krastin."

Thadd nodded.

Soon, Mal, Rhain, Thadd, and two fighters—Trist and Carvia—were running across the rocky landscape.

They dodged the lava pools, and the thin rivers of molten rock that crisscrossed the rocks.

Ahead, lay a foreboding rock formation. Black rocks arched up, sharp, pointed, and curved. They almost looked like the bones of some long-dead, giant creature.

There was no sign of the transport, or Krastin or Poppy.

But there were hexids.

A pair of the creatures loped out of the rocks. With a roar, they charged. Thadd chopped one down with his deadly sword. Rhain raised a palm and let off a pulse of energy.

The other hexid flew into the air and crashed down. The other two fighters ripped into it with their weapons.

Where the hell did Krastin go? Mal searched the rocks.

"This way," Rhain said.

"Look." Mal paused. There was a mouth of a cave that headed down into the ground under some rocks.

Into dark, impenetrable black.

"Did they go in there?" she asked.

Rhain nodded.

"We can't go in there." Thadd scowled, his sword resting up on his shoulder. "We have no idea what beasts are in there. It could be teeming with hexids and cupra."

Mal spun. "I have to find Poppy. She's *alive* and that asshole has her."

"She's a trap," Thadd said.

"You stay here then." Mal moved forward.

A flurry of curses echoed behind her, but the men and Carvia followed.

Mal's sword glowed silver, giving enough light to navigate. Rhain's swords gleamed red, Thadd's was gold, and Trist and Carvia's weapons were orange.

The rocky walls were black and jagged. Mal saw something in them and gasped. Old bones, fossils of long dead animals.

"Creatures that died in the Radiance," Rhain said.

The tunnel opened into an enormous cavern. Their light didn't penetrate far enough to see, but she felt a sense of enormous space.

"Do you feel anything?" she asked Rhain.

His brows drew together and he was tense. "No."

She took another step into the darkness and heard a growl. She froze.

Suddenly, two lights blinked on in the black.

Her chest locked. Not lights.

Eyes.

Gleaming eyes, like a sheen over oil.

A hexid.

More of them flickered on.

Dozens of them.

Mal lifted her sword, her heart thumping in her ears.

There were too many of them. There was no way they could fight them all and no way they could escape. The hexids would chase them down.

Thadd cursed. "No one ever listens to me."

Rhain's face was what she was starting to recognize as his king mask—cool, inscrutable.

She wanted to find Poppy, but she didn't want Rhain and his people to die here either. Energy began to pool around her. She called it to her. She had no idea how she was doing it, but it felt right.

Fueled by her emotions, the energy gathered around her, growing. She gasped. It felt so powerful. It made her feel powerful.

"We need to go," Thadd said.

"As soon as we move, they'll chase us," Rhain said.

Suddenly, several hexids launched forward.

They loped in, powerful bodies sprinting fast.

"Charge," Rhain yelled.

With a cry, Mal swung her sword. She sliced and stabbed, and saw other charged weapons glow brightly as the others fought. Rhain's red kilwar swords were a thing of breathtaking beauty. Thadd's sword looked like molten gold.

The first wave of hexids lay dead around them.

"Trist," Carvia cried.

The trim man had a glowing orange dagger in one hand and the other hand pressed to his shoulder. Blood seeped through his fingers from a nasty gash.

He made an annoyed male sound. "It's fine."

Carvia met Mal's gaze and rolled her eyes.

"Well done, Overlord."

The voice had them all whipping around. The power in Mal hurt, still growing, but she wrestled it down. A man stood on a rock, two hexids crouched beside him like pets.

It wasn't Krastin. Mal frowned, scanning the cave. No Poppy either. This tall, blond man was a stranger.

She heard Rhain suck in a sharp breath. He stared at the man, his jaw working.

"No matter how hard you fight, you will lose." The man smiled and spread his hands. "Give in to the might of King Zavir. It will be so much easier for you."

The man's skin looked burned on one side of his face. He had some sort of Zhylaw implant embedded in his neck. It looked new, the skin still red and raw around it.

"Rhain?" she asked quietly.

"He's Zhalton." Dark sorrow in his voice. And rage. "He's one of the dead from the Renkitis Outpost. We never found his body."

Her stomach cramped into sharp points. Krastin had taken this Zhalton man and twisted him into a puppet.

"I will never stand at Zavir's side." Rhain's voice echoed in the cavern. "And I will avenge you."

The Zhalton man shrugged. "He has a lot more planned to persuade you and your brothers, Overlord." He lifted a hand.

More hexids flooded out of the darkness. Hundreds of them. No, thousands.

They all howled, the sounds deafening.

Mal backed up, the others doing the same.

"There are too many," Thadd yelled.

"We fight," Rhain said grimly.

They'd all die. Mal watched Rhain lift his swords, his handsome face awash in red light.

Trist threw a dagger. It hit a hexid in the eye and the beast stumbled, tripping over several others.

The hexids would rip them to shreds. The thought of Rhain bloody and dying made her chest hollow out.

The energy in her swelled. She gasped. *Oh, man, it hurt.* She felt like she was on fire inside.

She shoved her sword back in its sheath and walked forward.

"Mal!" Rhain yelled.

She threw her palms up.

A giant wall of energy flared into existence between her and the hexids.

The creatures slammed into it, and it shimmered. But they couldn't get through.

Ow, that really hurt. Every hit reverberated through her.

"Auroras above," Thadd muttered.

On the other side of the energy wall, the altered Zhalton stared at her, wide-eyed.

"Mal?" Rhain moved in close behind her.

"Go." She had no idea how long she could hold it. She could feel the power draining out of her.

Every ram of the hexids weakened the wall.

"I can't... Hold it much longer. Go."

He stepped closer and she met his silver gaze. She wished she'd kissed him again. Gotten to spend more time with him.

"Promise me you'll find Poppy," she said.

He nodded.

"Now go."

His face twisted, and she felt his hand stroke down her back. She closed her eyes and absorbed the touch.

Then he stepped away.

Mal's awareness faded, her vision blurred.

The throb of her heartbeat was like a drum in her head, and she felt fluid leaking from her ears. Probably blood.

She'd die here, alone. She was sorry she couldn't save Poppy, but she thought Rhain would remember her. And at least he would live.

She threw her hands out once more, and there was a blast of energy as the wall gave way. Pain ripped through her, and she collapsed to the ground.

Then there was nothing.

RHAIN CAME to face down on hard rock.

He stifled a groan, aches and pains flaring in his body. He was alive, and nothing seemed to be broken, nor was he bleeding profusely.

He sat up and touched his head. His vision wavered. His temple and cheekbone were tender.

What had—?

Mal.

Pulse racing, Rhain pushed to his feet, searching frantically.

There.

She was laying on her side nearby.

He ran and dropped down beside her. "Mal?"

She was unconscious and covered in hexid blood, but when he saw her chest moving, he blew out a breath. He dropped down to sit beside her and pulled her into his arms.

After she'd thrown up that energy wall, he sent Thadd, Trist and Carvia back into the tunnel.

Then, at the last second, he'd used his abilities to collapse the roof... Between him and the others.

The last thing he'd seen was Thadd's furious face.

Yes, his captain of the guard would be very unhappy with Rhain.

Carefully he ran a hand over Mal's face. Courageous, foolish woman. So quick to sacrifice herself for others.

He lowered his forehead to hers and felt the warmth of her skin. He was so thankful she was alive.

He looked around. Faint light filtered in from above. The blast wave had caused some of the walls and part of the roof of the cavern to collapse. He saw a patch of light high above them.

Surrounding them were the bodies of dead hexids and nearby, he saw the Zhalton man.

The man was dead. His eyes stared lifelessly. Rhain felt the darkness inside him twist. The man was with the auroras now.

But his death had been needless.

Krastin and Zavir were to blame.

Rhain breathed through his rage. He stroked Mal's silky hair, trying to find a sense of calm.

A minute later, she stirred and her eyelids fluttered.

"Ugh, how much tequila did I drink?"

"Mal." Rhain brushed his fingers along her cheek.

Her eyes widened and she looked up at him. "Rhain."

She tilted her head and took in the dead hexid bodies. She grimaced. "Did I do that?"

"You saved our lives."

He helped her sit up and she leaned against him.

"I feel like I've had a bad case of the flu for three weeks. I've got no energy."

"You're burned out from the energy expenditure. It'll slowly replenish."

"Well, Rusty used to always tell me that if you're not hurting, you didn't try hard enough."

Rhain just grunted. He saw the instant she spotted the Zhalton man's body. Sorrow crossed her face.

"I'm sorry," she whispered.

"He's at peace now. But I will avenge him. Krastin. Will. Die."

At his tone, she frowned. "Hey." She cupped his cheek. "Turn down the scary."

Air shuddered out of Rhain. "I struggle with it."

"With what? You're entitled to be angry."

"It's more than that. My father's blood runs in me. The urge to fight, kill, and conquer." He looked away, couldn't look at her.

She snorted.

Shocked, Rhain whipped his head around.

"Rhain, you can be uber alpha sometimes, and bossy, but your people are free, happy, and prosperous. You're a good leader, and the total opposite of your asshole father."

Rhain frowned. "His blood runs in my veins."

"Maybe. But we aren't just genetics, or our parents. We make our own choices, and we all have secrets and things hiding in dark corners. But I know that you would never do this." She waved a hand at the dead hexids and altered Zhalton.

He cupped her jaw and forced her gaze to his. "I find you endlessly fascinating, Mallory West."

"You shouldn't. I'm not really that special."

He shook his head. "You're a loyal friend. Brave to the point of recklessness. You charge into fights to protect others with little thought for yourself. From what I've seen, you protect complete strangers."

"Rusty always taught me to help others." She rubbed her temple. "He had a saying about it, something about not standing on the sidelines, but hell I can't remember right now." She shrugged. "He taught me to always try to do the right thing, even when it was hard to do."

"I think I would've liked your Rusty."

She grinned. "I'm not sure he would've liked you. You're too fancy, and too rich, but he would've loved your swords." Then she frowned, gaze focused on his face. "You have a hell of a bruise coming up." She leaned closer and stroked the side of his eye.

It was tender. "I think I connected with a rock when the blast threw us."

She probed it gently, her lips tantalizingly close to his.

Her green-gold gaze flicked to his and she stilled.

"Mal, when we get out of here, I'm going to have you."

Heat flickered in her eyes—desire or anger, or perhaps a combination of both.

"Really?" she said.

"Yes. In my bed. I want to uncover every part of that tough body of yours. I want to lick you, kiss you, and discover what sounds you make when I sink my cock inside you."

She sucked in a breath and shifted. "Do I have a say in this?"

"Are you going to deny how you feel? I can see you squirming." He lowered his voice. "Are you wet for me?"

"*Rhain.*" She huffed out a breath. "This is crazy. You and me, it's crazy?"

"But it feels right." And it did. Too right.

"Fine," she said. "But I get to explore every inch of that big, muscled body of yours too." She leaned closer. "And I'll see what sounds *you* make when I'm riding your cock hard."

Her words had his cock harder than it had ever been before. He cupped the back of her head and kissed her.

She made a hungry sound, then nipped his bottom lip, and kissed him back.

When they pulled apart, his blood was humming, and he felt a trickle of energy seeping back into his body.

"Well." Mal cleared her throat. "With that motivation in mind, I guess we'd better find a way out of here."

He helped her up. "Are you feeling better?"

"I'd say your kiss is pretty potent, but I think your ego is healthy enough, Overlord."

"My energy is returning."

She nodded. "Mine too."

That's when Rhain felt a ripple of energy.

He turned, scanning the ruined cavern and saw

several hexids slink out of the shadows, their overlong arms flexing.

"We have company," he said quietly.

"These things never quit." She pulled her sword free of its scabbard.

Rhain did the same and looked up. "You think you can climb up to the opening above? Without falling?"

"A girl falls into a lake once and no one let's her live it down." She eyed the rock wall. "Well, if my options are stay in the dark hole with alien monsters or climb out, I'll climb."

Rhain charged his swords. "Good. First, let's deal with our new friends."

CHAPTER TEN

She officially hated hexids.

A big one ambled her way, upright, shoulders hunched, and its head cocked. Its dark eyes were filled with malice.

Mal's sword glowed, the white turning to brilliant silver. Energy flowed back through her—dulling her aches and pains, shoving her exhaustion aside.

Beside her, Rhain looked like some god of war come to pillage and plunder. He spun his glowing kilwar blades. Hot. The guy was so hot and he wanted her.

She'd decided he could have her.

But first...

"Shall we do this?" she asked.

The faint smile on his face just made him look hotter. He nodded.

Mal ran, leaped onto a rock, then jumped off it. Her sword sliced through the air and she cut through the first hexid, but another was on her in a blink.

She fell into a wild rhythm of cutting, slashing, and stabbing.

She thrust her sword into the hexid's chest. It bellowed, claws thrown wide. She twisted the blade and then pulled free.

Two hexids leapt off the rock, sprinting in her direction.

Rhain jumped in front of her. His powerful body fast and lethal. He cut down the hexids with powerful slashes.

The two of them kept fighting as more hexids rushed them. They ended up back to back, working together to take the enemy down.

Just like in their shared dream.

They moved as one unit. She whirled, and Rhain ducked and attacked. She slashed the side of the last hexid, and Rhain beheaded it.

"Nice work," she said.

"You too." Then he frowned, his head whipping around.

She felt it too. A ripple in the energy.

Something was coming.

"More hexids?" she asked.

He nodded. "Yes, but they seem...different."

The hexid that appeared was the same size as the others they'd fought, but this one was glowing molten red. Like it had dragged itself out of a lava pool.

More appeared, and even from a distance, she felt the heat emanating off them.

"Seriously?" she said. "They weren't bad enough already?"

Rhain's lips compressed into a firm line. "Krastin likes to experiment. These are blaze hexids. I've seen one once before. They are hot enough to melt your skin and bone."

"Lovely."

A blaze hexid moved toward them, picking up speed.

Rhain threw a hand out, and a blast of red energy pulsed through the air.

It hit the hexid and lifted it off its feet. It flew back and fell into the others.

More just walked over the top of their fallen comrades.

"We need to get out of here," Rhain said.

Mal nodded, then ran for the rock wall. Rhain was right behind her.

He let off another blast of energy, but the blaze hexids kept coming.

She grabbed his hand and raised her other palm.

"Together," she said.

He nodded.

They spun and released a dual blast of energy. Red and silver twined together.

It hit the hexids like a tidal wave, and they slammed into the far wall.

Then...*boom*.

Rhain swiveled and shielded her with his body, pressing her against the rock.

Mal felt a wash of intense heat.

"Are you okay?" she cried.

He gave her a clipped nod. "Climb. *Now*."

Turning, she started up the rock wall. There were

lots of handholds, but also lots of loose rocks, which made it slippery. She clung to the wall, moving slowly and steadily. Soon her arm and leg muscles started to burn, but she kept moving upward.

The patch of blue sky got bigger. When she pulled herself out of the cavern, she smiled.

Thank God.

They weren't where they'd entered it. They were on higher ground, with the perfect view of the Barrens spreading out in all its rocky glory.

Rhain sank down next to her, breathing heavily.

She frowned. "Rhain?"

Lines bracketed his mouth, and his bronze skin was pale.

Her heart leaped into her throat. "Rhain, what's wrong?" She shifted closer to him.

And saw his back.

He was burned badly. From the blast. Her gut curdled. From shielding her.

"You idiot!" She bent over him and touched his shoulder blade. His armor was melted in patches, and his skin was burned. In places, the metal was embedded in his skin. It had to be agony.

"What can I do?" She slid her hand around and stroked his jaw.

"Nothing." He pulled in a shuddering breath. "We need to get out of here."

He needed a damn medica.

Panic, hot and slick, filled her throat. There was nothing close by but rocks.

Wait.

She blinked. Those weren't rocks. It was a Zhylaw raider ship parked close by.

"Come on, your Overlordness. I've found our ride home."

She helped him up, which wasn't easy. She got his arm around her shoulders and she almost collapsed under the weight of him. The man was solid muscle.

Together, they hobbled toward the ship. When he saw it, he groaned.

"You can't fly that."

"Watch me."

As they neared the small ship, the dark glass canopy over the cockpit opened automatically.

Handy. Two black seats sat at the front, and the jagged back end really did look like the teeth of some giant monster. It was made of black matte metal.

She got Rhain into one of the seats. He dwarfed it.

"I take it the Zhylaw are small?"

He nodded, his eyes looking unfocused from the pain.

She settled into the pilot's seat and stared at the control panel.

Uh-oh. It was filled with loads of black, jagged switches and levers. There were no labels—which wouldn't have helped her anyway.

Oh, well. Flying was flying. She'd work it out.

She tapped at the switches, trying to assess what everything did. With the next press, the engine started.

Yes. Now they were cooking.

Rhain groaned. "You'll kill us."

"Have a little faith." She glanced up and her muscles stiffened.

Several blaze hexids were running their way.

Crap.

She pressed a button and the glass canopy of the cockpit closed. A few more presses, and the ship shot forward, scraping over the rocky ground.

Oops. There was an obvious controller, similar to a joystick, and she pulled on it. The ship's nose lifted.

They flew into the air.

"Hell, yeah." She gently slapped Rhain's arm. "I told you."

He gave her a faint smile. "We need to head that way." He pointed to the right.

It took Mal a few tries, which included some wobbly dips and stomach-shaking vibration, to set the path to Citadel.

God, it was nice to be back in the air.

"When we get back, you can enjoy Tavith bitching at you while he heals you," she said.

Rhain gave a choked laugh. "Remember, I want you in my bed, Mal."

Flames ignited in her belly. "I haven't forgotten."

His look warned her that the man had plans.

She glanced away, then she gasped. "Rhain, look."

Ahead were endless green flower fields. And in the distance, the mountains of Citadel.

Suddenly, lights started blinking on the console and a strident noise filled the cockpit. She assumed it was an alarm.

"What's wrong?" she cried.

"I don't know." He groaned, looking paler.

Then, the ship's engine died.

Mal's stomach dropped to her boots. "Are you strapped in?" She leaned over, checking him.

His eyes were narrow slits. He was barely holding onto consciousness.

"Hold on, Rhain."

He managed a nod.

She checked his harness, then she turned back to the controls. She needed to baby the ship so—

The nose dropped.

Oh, fuck.

She started yanking on the controller, trying all the levers. "Three crashes in a week, really?"

Rhain slumped beside her. She tried all the controls and watched helplessly as they lost altitude.

She didn't want to die. She didn't want Rhain to die.

The ground got closer and closer and she braced.

They slammed into a field, dirt spraying over the cockpit windshield. Then she was tossed forward and it was lights out.

MAL WOKE AND GROANED. She felt wrung out, beyond exhausted, but not in agony.

She remembered the crash. *What happened after that?*

She dragged in a breath and smelled Rhain. She opened her eyes and saw him lying beside her on a big bed. He was asleep, resting on his side, facing her. That masculine face still looked hard and rugged in sleep.

Pushing up on one elbow, she realized that she was wearing a loose shirt that was way too big for her. The bedroom was huge and full of light. There were smooth stone floors, loads of green plants in pots, and a big bed that dominated the space. There was an interesting string instrument resting in one corner. His kilwar blades hung on the wall, and she saw her sword and scabbard resting on a wooden dresser.

Rhain's bedroom.

She looked back at him. His dark hair was stark against the white pillow. She touched his bare arm. He felt warm.

She leaned over to check his burned back, but there was no sign of his terrible injuries. Air shuddered out of her. *Thank God.*

"Welcome back."

Tavith.

Mal swiveled and watched the medica hurry in.

"You are really testing my healing abilities," he huffed.

"Sorry." Her voice was croaky.

"Somehow I don't think you are." He lifted his wrist and scanned her, studying the projection. He grunted.

"What happened?"

"You held back a wave of hexids, then let loose with a huge energy blast, fought some blaze hexids, and then decided to crash a Zhylaw ship."

"It was a slow day." She winced. "I feel like I've been pummeled by rocks."

"Our illustrious overlord came to for a bit when we reached the crash site and told us what happened. I've never seen the captain of the guard so angry."

"I don't know, angry seems Thadd's standard mode."

"Rhain demanded we bring you here, to his room, and heal you, even though he was badly injured."

She stiffened, her gaze dropping to his face. "Is he okay?"

"He's still unconscious, but he's fine."

Suddenly, the doors were flung open and a woman in a blue dress strode in. Her brown hair was piled up in a complicated design. Her bearing was regal and elegant, and her eyes were a brilliant blue.

Two guards wearing red sashes stood by a door, eyeing the woman with uncertain looks. Tavith nodded at them and they closed the doors.

"Countess Naveri." Tavith bowed his head.

Mal yanked the sheet up to her chest.

"Is this the woman my adopted son risked his life for?" She spoke in smooth, even tones.

"Yes, Mallory West, Countess Naveri."

"Hi." Was she supposed to curtsey or something?

The woman sniffed and looked at Rhain. "Is he all right? When will he wake up?"

"His vitals are fine," Tavith said. "He should wake soon, I hope. It's hard to tell."

The woman made a sound.

Mal looked up at her. It was clear she cared for Rhain. "I didn't mean for him to get hurt. I told him to leave me."

The countess sniffed. "So Thadd told me."

Thadd. Mal realized the woman had Thadd's eyes. His mother.

"I'm looking for my best friend." And now Krastin had Poppy. Mal felt sick. God, was Poppy okay? The guy was a psychopath, from everything she'd heard.

"I understand." The countess' gaze softened a fraction. "Rhain's mother was my best friend."

The medica cleared his throat. "For now, the overlord and Mallory need some rest."

The countess' blue gaze zeroed in on Mal. Mal fought the urge to fidget and held it.

"Very well. I would like to be informed when he awakens." With another piercing, unreadable look, the older woman swept out.

"Does she practice entering and exiting a room like that?" Mal wondered.

Tavith's lips quirked. "Now, I want you to rest."

"I think—"

He held up a hand. "No. Just resting. Don't get up. Don't fight a hexid. Don't fly an alien ship. Stay in this bed."

She heaved a sigh. "Fine." She really didn't want more lectures.

"Good. I'll check on you in a few hours."

Mal lay down beside Rhain, taking in his dark, thick lashes. "Hey, your Overlordness, it'd be good if you opened those eyes."

His eyelashes fluttered.

"Come on, Rhain, please don't just lie around. That's lazy. We have an alien warlord to take down."

He opened one eye. "Lazy?"

She gasped and sat up. "You're awake?"

"For a few minutes. I was waiting for the countess to leave."

Mal snorted. "You're king of an entire planet, but you're afraid of your adopted mom?"

A faint smile on his lips. "Afraid is a strong word. She lectures. A lot. Especially when she's upset. I wanted to avoid that."

Mal brushed his fingers. They curled around hers.

"Are you okay?" she asked quietly.

"Yes, just a headache. You?"

She nodded.

"You don't like seeing me get hurt," he murmured.

She looked down, her heart thudding. "I guess not."

"Come closer, Mal."

He sat up, the sheet pooling at his waist.

Oh boy. She'd never seen a better bare chest. He was perfectly proportioned, with gorgeous tan skin, and lots of lean muscle.

"I don't like seeing you hurt, either," he said. "Now, I promised you that when we got back here, you were mine."

Desire flared inside her, scalding hot. "You're hurt."

"No, I was hurt. Now, I'm all healed." He loomed closer.

"Rhain—"

She didn't get to finish. Rhain moved and Mal found herself flat on her back, with him on top of her.

His mouth hit hers and then he was kissing her.

Yes. Heat pumped off him. She made a sound, gripped his arms and deepened the kiss.

He angled his head, tongue plunging. She made a hungry, muffled sound, desire unfurling. It drenched her, leaving her on fire.

His hands skimmed her body, then fisted in the loose shirt she wore. He broke the kiss to rip it off her and she lifted her arms to help.

Then she was naked.

He pushed up, his gaze traveling over her. One hand cupped her breast and he made a hungry sound in his throat. Then he lowered his head. He peppered kisses down her neck, across her collarbone.

Mal moaned his name, her nails scraping down his back. Then he lifted her breast and his tongue teased her nipple before he sucked it into his mouth.

"*Oh.*" She'd never really found her breasts that sensitive before, but now, with Rhain's mouth on them, sensation shot straight between her legs.

She writhed on the bed. He shifted and lavished the other breast with the same attention. His mouth drifted lower. As he'd promised, he explored every inch of her. Her skin felt hot as he moved down her body, licking, nipping, stopping at every dip and curve that took his interest. He was seducing her, driving her mad with need.

He took his time on her belly button, his teeth raking across her hipbone. He ran his hands up her body, his long fingers shaping her torso. She felt the scrape of his calluses on her skin.

"*Mal.*" His voice was hoarse, and he looked mesmerized by his hands on her. Darker bronze against creamy gold.

She ran her hands across his muscular shoulders. For the first time in her life, she felt small, feminine. He made her feel like that, when they were alone.

Out there, she saw how he reveled in her strength.

No man had ever looked at her like that. No man had ever seen all sides of her.

She moved her hands to his chest. He felt like rock. She flicked her nail over one of his flat nipples.

She felt his muscles ripple, and he made a deep sound. He pushed her thighs apart.

She'd waxed not long before her test flight. She had a thin strip of hair and he seemed fascinated by it, his fingers stroking her. Her hips lifted.

He lowered his head and she felt his hot breath on her inner thighs. She writhed, but he pressed a palm to her lower belly. He licked the plump flesh between her legs.

Crying out, Mal surged up.

"I'm going to make you scream, Mal," he growled.

That delicious mouth was a sensual assault. He licked and sucked, the deep groans he made leaving no doubt he was enjoying every second.

His tongue stabbed deep and she moaned.

Then his tongue brushed her clit and she cried out.

Rhain lifted his head. His thumb found the swollen nub and rubbed.

"Oh, *God*."

"This gives you pleasure?"

"Yes." She panted. "Are women different here?"

"Yes, the center of their pleasure is just inside." He thrust a finger inside her.

She moaned. "That feels good too, but it's more concentrated at my clit, um, clitoris."

He made a sound, his finger moving back to rub her clit. He looked fascinated. The sounds coming from her turned incoherent. She thrashed, pleasure a wild flood in her belly.

He watched her, his face filled with arousal. "How do you like to be caressed? Tell me."

She gasped. "Your mouth. Use your mouth."

He lowered his head again, and this time, his lips closed around her clit.

"*Oh...*" She wasn't going to last long. He suckled and licked.

As her orgasm hit, bright and hot, she screamed his name. Waves of pleasure washed over her. Her body shook, the ecstasy drowning her.

When he kept sucking, she gently pushed his mouth away.

"I can't... It's too sensitive." Her body shivered through the aftershocks of pleasure.

He sat back on his knees. He had a thick, long cock that was hard and erect. *Oh, boy.* She couldn't look away. It was beautiful.

She had the faint thought that it was lucky she had a contraceptive implant, because if anyone could get her pregnant, it would be this virile alien king.

Rhain gripped her thighs and yanked her closer.

Oh, God. He circled his cock and brought it between her spread legs. She sucked in a breath, excitement shooting through her.

"Mal, look at me," he growled.

She ripped her gaze off his cock and met his eyes.

Her belly contracted. The look on his face was indescribable.

Then she felt the head of his cock brush her. With one firm thrust, he buried himself inside her.

Mal moaned. Rhain was inside her. The two of them, now one. Nothing in her entire life had ever felt so right. She'd never been one with anyone before. Never really belonged anywhere.

She arched her back, pressing her head back into the bed. Then Rhain started thrusting.

He wasn't gentle, but it wasn't more than she could handle. He was strength and power, and she wanted it all.

Her eyes drifted closed.

"*Mal.*" His voice a gritty growl. "Watch me. Watch me fucking you."

"God, Rhain." A whimper slipped from her. She'd never, ever get enough of this.

"You want more, Mal?"

"I want all of you. Don't hold back." She lifted her hips, meeting his heavy thrusts. "I can take you."

"Yes," he growled. "You can take everything."

He pulled out and she cried out.

"*No.*"

Then he flipped her over onto her belly. Her hands gripped the sheets and she felt that big body straddle her.

"Rhain—"

He lifted her hips and pushed back inside her.

Oh. *God.* His thrusts were heavy and deep. She moaned against the bed.

Rhain gripped her hair, turning her head, even as his body kept possessing hers. He leaned down and kissed her.

"You're so tight and hot, Mal. Perfect and all mine."

"*Yes*."

She felt the pulse of energy around them—hers and his. It swelled, mixed, and seemed to heighten everything.

Then she felt his hand slide under her body. He found her clit, his cock still slamming into her. He pinched the swollen nub and it threw her straight into another orgasm.

She screamed against the bed. Sensation, hot and strong, cut through her. Energy seared over her skin, making everything *more*. It felt never-ending, the pleasure too much, but oh-so-good. Wave after wave of sensation washed through her.

Rhain's loud grunts filled her ears as he drove deep one last time. He ground against her ass as he came, his big body shuddering.

Mal was breathing harshly, not sure she'd ever move again. He dropped down beside her, still half on her, and she liked the solid weight of him.

He nuzzled her face and kissed her. "Now I know the sounds you make when you take my cock."

"So romantic," she murmured. She felt limp, lazy, and too good to move.

"You want romance?" he asked.

"No, I want you to fuck me like that again. Later, once I've recovered some feeling in my extremities."

His low chuckle was damned attractive.

"Tavith said I had to stay in bed and rest," she said. "I'm pretty sure this wasn't what he had in mind."

Another chuckle.

Mal curled on her side, suddenly tired. Rhain shifted and wrapped his big body protectively around hers.

She barely noticed him pulling the covers over them. Warm, safe, and sated, sleep pulled her under.

CHAPTER ELEVEN

Rhain nodded at his guards and slipped quietly back into his bedroom.

He'd left Mal exhausted and fast asleep in the center of his bed. He smiled to himself, careful not to spill anything off the tray of food he'd grabbed from the kitchen. His very surprised kitchen night staff had sprung into action to prepare a late-night feast for him.

He and Mal had burned off lots of energy and needed to replenish.

After that first intense time taking her, he'd had her two more times. That body of hers... She was fit, flexible, and had stamina. She didn't hold back. She showed him the full force of how much she desired him, not once shying away from what he wanted to do to her.

He silently crossed the room, which was drenched in shadows only lit by the auroras shining outside. That's when he saw the bed was empty.

His pulse jumped.

Then he heard the faint strum of the lila. He noted

the instrument was missing from the corner where he usually kept it.

He turned and noticed a door to his balcony was open.

Still carrying the tray, he followed the sound of the music, and stepped outside.

He spotted her instantly, felt her energy—bright and clean. She was lying on one of the large, square outdoor pillows that dotted the balcony. He often sat out here at night, when he couldn't sleep, and watched the auroras as he worked through whatever problems kept him awake.

She was holding the lila wrong—more tilted to the side—but the slow, melancholy music she was making was incredible.

"I thought you'd still be sleeping," he said.

Her fingers stilled and she turned on the pillow. She wore one of his black shirts. It was too big for her, and she'd left it unfastened. He saw a tantalizing strip of tan skin up the center of her body.

"The bed was empty without you."

"I went to get us some sustenance." He set the tray down, then shifted in to sit beside her. She leaned back against him.

Mal West leaning on him. He liked that.

"I hope it was okay to use this," she said.

"Yes. I barely ever use it. My mother forced lila lessons on me when I was a child."

"Lila." She rolled the word around. "I have a guitar. *Had* a guitar. It's similar to this."

"You play well." He fingered her silky hair. He liked it loose like this. "Play me something else."

With a small smile, she stroked the strings, playing a lovely song with a slow beat. He watched the way her eyes closed and she lost herself to the music. He liked seeing her like this—relaxed, at ease.

Finally, the song ended.

"The auroras are so pretty tonight." She sighed. "There's pink shot through parts of them."

He stroked her hair, once again marveling at how soft it was. "You're thinking of Poppy."

Mal nodded. "Here I am having hot sex with a hot alien king, and she's..."

"Hey." He gripped her chin and made her look at him. "You will not feel guilty about what's between us. We *will* find Poppy, but right now, we have no idea where she is."

Mal's face hardened. "If Krastin's hurt her, I'll..."

"Krastin is *mine*."

She rose, setting the lila aside. She paced the balcony, agitated. "He wants to kill you."

"My father wants me alive."

"I don't think Krastin cares. He'll kill you, and tell your father it was a tragic accident."

"I can hold myself against Krastin."

She threw out a hand. "Says the man who was badly injured just hours ago."

"This is *my* planet, *my* people. They are mine to protect."

She ground her teeth together. "I think this is more personal than that. It's about your mother."

"Of course, it is."

She spun to face him. "If you go into a fight with your emotions running high, you'll get hurt, or killed."

"Zavir my father. He's a *gorr*, power-hungry. He doesn't care how many people he kills. I have to stop him."

"To prove you aren't like him?"

"Yes."

"I don't believe that for a second. We're more than the genetic material of our parents, Rhain. I have no idea who my father was. He was a deadbeat dad who didn't stick around. That's what I came from."

Rhain rose. "That power-hungry need for more, to kill to protect what's mine. It's what drives my father. And I feel it, too." He turned and met her gaze. "That's what my father gave me. I fight it every day."

"Rhain." She moved to him, rested her hands on his chest. "You could *never* become your father."

"I hope not, for all our sakes."

"Rusty used to say that we always know the right thing, but the hard part is doing it. Most things in life aren't easy, Rhain. We're always considering, weighing, and hoping we get it right. You're surrounded by good people to help you do that. Thadd and your fighters would die for you. Thadd's mom would kill for you."

He tucked her hair behind her ear. "Does that include you?"

She went up on her toes and kissed him. "I guess it does."

The kiss deepened and he wrapped an arm around her. He tugged her closer and squeezed her ass.

She hummed into his mouth. "You know, I promised

to find out what sounds you made when I was riding you hard." A feminine smile curled her lips. "You haven't given me the chance yet."

He hadn't. His need had been so great, all he'd been able to do was pin her down and thrust inside her tight body.

She nudged him back a few steps and urged him down. He sank onto the pillow.

Rhain opened his legs and she knelt between them. No woman had ever looked more beautiful—desire on her face, the light of the auroras on her skin.

She leaned over him, that shirt hanging open to give him a pretty view of her bare breasts. She kissed his neck, her hands sliding along his shoulders to push his shirt off.

"God, this chest." She kissed across his pecs, her tongue laving first one nipple, then the other.

Rhain bit back a groan.

She traveled downward, then she pushed the waistband of his silky, black shorts down and pulled out his hard cock.

It was already throbbing. Rock-hard at the thought of her sinking down on it.

She made a hungry sound and pumped it.

"What now, Mal?" His voice was guttural.

"Don't rush me. I want to taste you first."

His cock jumped at the thought of her mouth wrapped around it. She lowered her head and licked.

He cursed. He leaned back as she licked, sucked, and bobbed her head. Her mouth was warm and she was clearly enjoying herself.

Any more of this and he'd come in her mouth.

He tangled a hand in her hair and tugged her up. "You won't hear the sounds I make when you ride me if you don't stop now."

Licking her lips, her face flushed, she moved up to straddle him.

Finally. His abs contracted.

She notched his cock between her thighs, then her gaze locked with his, and she lowered herself down.

Auroras above. He growled. "Take me, Mal. So tight."

She gripped his shoulders, her teeth sinking into her bottom lip.

"Ride me," he ordered.

She did. She moved up and down, and soon he was bucking his hips up, trying to go deeper.

He cupped one of her breasts, listening to the slap of their bodies and the panting of their breath.

"Faster, Mal."

"*God*, baby." She arched her back. "You're so big and I'm so full of you."

He gripped her hip, then moved lower. He found that fascinating little nub. Her clit. He rolled it.

With a low moan, she moved faster.

"Mal." He felt his release coming, rolling in like a storm.

"*Rhain*." She thrust down and started coming.

He leaned forward and took her mouth.

With a low roar, he bucked up and poured himself inside her.

When he could think, see, and hear again, he was lying on his back on the pillow, Mal sprawled on top of him. His semi-soft cock was still inside her, and her breath was puffing against his neck.

He lazily stroked a hand up her back. "Now you know."

She laughed. "Only a little. I was too busy with my own orgasm to hear all the sounds you made." She lifted her head, eyes sparkling. "Guess we'll just have to do it again."

He pulled her closer. "I guess I can suffer through, somehow."

She pinched his arm.

"Are you hungry?" he asked.

"Are we talking about food now?"

"Yes."

"Then, yes, I'm starving."

He shifted to sit up. "Then I'd better feed my woman."

As she smiled and tried the Zhalton delicacies he'd brought for her, Rhain knew this time—just the two of them, alone—was borrowed.

When the morning came, Krastin would once again overshadow everything.

And soon, they'd both wade back into a dangerous fight.

But one thing was for sure—Rhain no longer just fought to protect his people. He'd also fight for this Earth woman who'd crashed into his world and changed everything.

THE NEXT MORNING, Tavith dragged a reluctant Mal out of Rhain's room.

"I need to run more tests on you, and assess how your changes due to the Zhalton environment are progressing."

"Maybe later, Tavith, I—"

"Now," the medica said.

Rhain finished fastening his shirt. "Go with him, Mal."

She sniffed. She wore fitted pants, and a tight, blue shirt that left her toned arms bare. It showcased her strength.

"Fine. But if you hear anything about Poppy, I want to know straight away."

Rhain walked to her and cupped her cheek. "Of course." He dropped a kiss to her lips and was fascinated to see color fill her cheeks.

She cleared her throat and shot a look at Tavith.

"He's a medica, Mal, I'm pretty certain he knows what we've been doing in here."

"Resting," Tavith said, voice deadpan.

"I stayed in bed," she said. "Mostly."

"Go and get checked." Rhain tugged on her ponytail and looked past her to Tavith. "Her energy is strong. It glows silver-white."

The medica's eyes widened. "Really?"

"She threw up the strongest energy wall I've seen. Her skills are different than Zhaltons."

"Due to her different genetic material." Tavith focused on her. "Let's go. I'm eager to get to work."

She shot Rhain a resigned look as the medica pulled her out the door.

Rhain found a stone-faced Thadd waiting for him outside.

"Your advisors are waiting." The captain's tone was cool.

They fell into step.

"Any word from the scouts?" Rhain asked.

Thadd shook his head. "Nothing."

Rhain let out a breath. *Gorr*, they needed to find Krastin. "Thadd, I'm sorry. For blocking you in the cavern. I had to help Mal."

"It's my job, my *duty*, to protect you."

"I know and I stopped you from doing that."

"You risked your life for her."

Oh, his captain was not happy. "Yes. And she risked hers to save all of us."

"You're the overlord. She is...not even Zhalton."

"She's *mine* now." Rhain stopped and faced his friend.

"So sleep with her and be done with it." Thadd tossed a frustrated hand in the air. "Don't risk your life for her."

"Thadd," Rhain growled. "You will protect her like you protect me."

Thadd's mouth tightened. He looked like he wanted to hit something.

"She is *mine*."

Finally, Thadd nodded. He might not be happy, but if there was one thing that Rhain could count on, it was Thadd's bone-deep loyalty.

They entered the main chamber. Jaro and several advisors, including some nobles, waited for him.

"Overlord." Jaro bowed his head. "We're very happy to see you healthy and looking so refreshed."

Being refreshed had nothing to do with his healing and everything to do with Mal. "Did you recover the downed flyer and our people without incident?"

"Yes." Jaro turned and a projection flared up. "We tracked the Zhylaw raiders to a location close to the cavern where you fought the hexids."

Rhain turned back to the projection. "We need to find Krastin's base."

"We've doubled the number of scouts in the area, my lord," Jaro said. "But as you know, it is very rough terrain."

"Krastin's taunting us, trying to lure you out," Thadd said. "He wants you dead."

"My father doesn't want me dead." Zavir wanted to use Rhain and his power.

"Krastin will kill you, claim it was an accident, and beg for forgiveness."

"That's what Mal said."

"For once, I agree with her."

There was the sound of the swish of skirts, and Rhain tensed. He knew that sound. Across from him, Thadd stiffened.

Two young women in long, white dresses stepped into the room. One had waist-length, blonde hair, and the other had deep-red hair.

"Overlord," the blonde murmured.

They both bowed their heads. They wore crowns of flowers on their heads and no shoes.

"Our mistress requests your presence," the blonde said.

"And the newcomer," the redhead added.

"Newcomer?" Rhain asked.

"The female who crashed on our planet."

Mal.

Rhain really didn't want to take her to see the priestess. But he didn't have much of a choice. The priestesses of energy had been around since the Radiance. Most people called the head priestess an energy witch.

No one really practiced religion on Zhalto, but everyone revered the energy that infused their lives. No one dared anger or insult the energy priestesses.

He'd learned early on that ignoring the energy witch only caused more problems.

"Very well."

The two young women bowed and glided away.

Thadd cleared his throat. "I have some things to do. You'll be safe at the temple, so I'll see you when you return."

"Coward."

"Yes." Thadd stalked off.

Rhain headed down the hall toward the medica ward. He found Mal sitting on a bunk while Tavith scanned her.

"Is she okay?" he asked.

The medica nodded. "Fit and healthy. Her body is still adapting to the environment, so she may still manifest some new energy abilities, but other than that, she's fine."

Mal jumped off the bunk. "Great."

"We have a visit to make," Rhain told her.

She raised a brow.

"The head priestess has summoned us."

Beside her, Tavith did his best to hide a wince.

"Priestess?" Mal said.

"Yes, we have a sect of women who are especially sensitive to energy. Most people call them energy witches. They can see visions."

Both of Mal's eyebrows went up. "Really?"

"Really. They connect with the energy flowing somehow between space and time, and get glimpses of the future."

"O-*kay*."

"The head priestess might give us something about Krastin or Poppy."

Mal froze. "All right. Lead on."

They headed out of the palace and crossed the large main bridge. He watched Mal slow her steps, breathe deeply.

"God, this place is pretty."

He looked at it, trying to see it through her eyes. "I loved growing up here. I grew up running through the streets of Citadel with Thadd."

"He's like a brother to you."

"I also have two brothers."

Her eyebrows winged up. "Really?"

"Not here. They aren't Zhalton, and they're technically half-brothers. Zavir fathered a son with wives from the other two habitable planets in the system. My brother Brodin rules the planet Damar. Graylan rules the planet Taln."

"Do you get along?"

He nodded. "We do, and we're united in our hatred of Zavir."

"Can they use energy like you do?"

"No, each of the species on the other planets have their own powers. The Damari are wolf shapeshifters, and the Taln can utilize the geological forces of their planet." He scanned his city. "I worry that Zavir will attack their planets too."

She touched Rhain's arm. "You'll beat him."

A group of children, led by two teachers, walked by. The boys and girls called out hellos and waved to Rhain, all of them beaming.

"You belong here." A sad smile crossed Mal's face. "It must be nice to know you truly fit somewhere."

He hated that she'd never had that. "I always knew Zavir might come for me, or attack Zhalto. I knew I had to protect it."

"I get that...but at what price?"

"Any."

She looked away. "Your own life?"

"If required." He moved closer behind her, nuzzled her neck. "But I'd prefer to live."

She looked up at him. "I'd prefer that too."

He took her hand, entwining their fingers. He led her toward the temple of the energy.

It was built of the same white stone as the palace, but more intricately carved.

"God, it looks like icing," Mal muttered. "Like a fancy cake."

They entered through the large, arched doorway. Several young women in flowing, gauzy dresses of white and pale blue met them.

Inside, there were flowers everywhere. They were all pale colors as well, energy wafting off them.

A tall brunette appeared, her hair flowing to her waist. "She's waiting for you, Overlord."

"Thank you."

They entered through another ornate archway. Beyond lay a shadowed room, candles flickering, creating islands of light. A shallow pool of water sat in the center. Light filtered down from above, making the surface shine silver.

A woman stepped forward.

The witch was a few years older than Rhain. Tall, slender, with a wisp of a white dress on, she had long, dark hair that fell below her hips.

She was beautiful, but the constant immersion in the energy left her thin, brittle, her cheekbones like blades.

She wore a single, silver flower tucked behind one ear. Her eyes were so silver that they looked white, sparking with electricity.

Beside him, he felt Mal stiffen.

"Overlord." The woman's voice held a faint, sibilant rasp.

"Priestess."

The woman turned her eerie gaze to Mal. "Mallory West of Earth."

"Ah, nice to meet you."

"You've come a long way."

"Accidentally."

"I sense you are where you're supposed to be."

Mal glanced at Rhain, then back at the woman. "I have to find my friend."

"Yes, before it's too late."

Mal took a step forward. "Do you know something? Is Poppy all right?"

"She has a difficult journey ahead."

"Um, do you give straight answers?"

The woman spread long-fingered hands. "I share what the energy shares with me."

Mal released a long breath. "Okay."

"Overlord, you must face Krastin. The prosperity of Zhalto depends on it."

"How do we find him?" Rhain asked.

"I don't know all the answers. Some, you will have to uncover for yourself."

He winced.

"Rhain?" Mal said.

"She wants to do a vision."

"What does that mean?" Mal asked.

"You must both step into the energy." The priestess touched her finger to the pool of water.

A blast of energy filled the room, and the water flew up, then fell back down into the pool.

Mal gasped and stepped backward.

Energy rose like a mist, twisting around the pool and into the air. It looked like a whirlwind, sparking with different colors.

"We have to step into that?" Mal breathed.

"It won't hurt you," he said. "But it's not pleasant."

"You've done it before?"

"A few times."

"Well, if it helps us find Poppy..."

He held out his hand and she took it.

Together they stepped into the energy maelstrom.

CHAPTER TWELVE

Oh. *God.*

It was like stepping into a vortex. Energy whipped around Mal and stung her skin. She wondered how long she would have to endure the discomfort.

Then, suddenly, it seemed to flow more evenly, like it was adjusting itself to her.

Strong fingers squeezed hers, and she looked up into silver eyes. She loved looking at those eyes.

Rhain pulled her closer, and she wrapped her arms around him.

Images hammered at her brain, like flashes of light, too fast to comprehend.

She saw Rhain. She saw Krastin. She saw Poppy.

She saw herself and Rhain in the garden. Naked. His big hands on her body.

Desire swamped her.

She looked up and saw that his eyes were glowing, and she felt the throb between her legs.

She went up on her toes and kissed him.

It was wild, hungry. He hauled her closer. The energy enhanced it all, but she knew Rhain was potent enough without it.

They kissed in the center of the energy storm, and nothing had ever felt more right.

Mal felt truly connected to him, not alone, like she was important to this man.

Then slowly, the energy died away.

They broke the kiss, and stood there staring at each other.

The energy witch laughed. "Energy loves to transform and change, kill and unite."

Great, more useless drivel.

"What did you see?" Rhain asked the witch, his voice husky.

"You two are connected. Where you are supposed to be."

"Poppy?" Mal prompted. "How do we find her?"

"Follow the pull. You are sensitive to the energy, Mallory West, open yourself."

She felt something in her chest, a faint tug. She rubbed her breastbone.

The witch smiled. "*Yes.*"

"Thank you, Priestess," Rhain said.

"I know you dislike visiting me, Overlord."

"Not you, the visions."

"Because you're a man who likes to forge his own way. It is not incompatible. The future is always fluid, but some things are harder to change. Your own actions will define you." She paused. "You may find your friend changed, Mal. She'll need your help."

"What does that mean?" Mal asked.

The glow in the witch's eyes dimmed. "That's all the energy has shown me. Go now."

Mal walked out with Rhain. When they stepped into the sunshine, she blinked.

"Well, that was interesting."

He touched her cheek. "Are you all right?"

"I think so."

"It often makes little sense at first."

She rubbed her eyes. "It's all a confusing jumble..." She turned, and her chest throbbed.

"What?" he asked.

"I do feel, like, a pressure. Like I want to head in a certain direction."

"Where?"

She swiveled. "East."

Rhain sucked in a breath. "Do you think that you're sensing your friend in the energy field?"

"I have no idea. Maybe? I mean, I can't do that on Earth."

"But you appear to be very energy sensitive, and here, you have new abilities."

"We don't have anything to lose following this compulsion," she said.

"Then let's plan a trip back to the Barrens and see where it leads us."

After that, everything became a whirlwind of preparation. Back at the palace, Rhain barked orders, and his advisors and fighters snapped into action.

"It's best if we first head to the Emex Outpost," Thadd said.

Back in the planning room, they stood by the circular table.

"Do we fly to the outpost?" someone asked.

The captain shook his head. "I suggest we take the ruggers. The flyers are too hard to hide, and emit too much energy. I think that's how the Zhylaw found us before."

"What is this outpost?" Mal asked.

"A heavily fortified mining outpost," Rhain said. "They have an energy shield."

She nodded. "Sounds like a good base of operations."

"Let's assemble the team," Rhain said. "Our best fighters."

Back in Rhain's room, Mal quickly showered and changed. Someone had delivered new armor for her, and she pulled it over her chest. She strapped on her sword.

Whatever she had to do to find Poppy, she'd do it.

Two tan-colored ruggers waited outside the palace. Rhain stood beside one, talking with some of his advisors. He caught her gaze and nodded.

Trist leaned against the second one, sharpening a dagger. He winked at her.

When she boarded the rugger, she found a team of tough, rugged fighters already on board. They all eyed her with flat eyes, taking her measure. She was well aware that if she posed a risk to Rhain, they'd cut her down without any hesitation.

Rhain stepped aboard, nodding to his people. He sat beside her.

An unfamiliar sensation moved through her. She

didn't want him hurt. She was starting to feel way too much for this man.

As they journeyed away from Citadel, she looked out the reinforced window and watched the farmland pass by. The land slowly began to get rockier and rougher.

Then she saw the shadows of the Badus Mountains.

Mal bounced her foot.

"It isn't too far to the outpost from here," Rhain said. "It's on the boundary with the Barrens."

"What do they mine?"

"A metal called craxma. It's extremely strong and durable."

Suddenly, the rugger rocked violently.

Boom.

The whole vehicle shuddered, and turned sharply.

"Thadd!" Rhain yelled.

They rocked to a stop.

The captain leaped up out of his seat. "We've hit a mine field. Someone's put explosives in the ground."

Rhain cursed. "Krastin."

"The other rugger got hit."

Rhain reached up and opened the top hatch of the rugger. He jumped up and climbed up the short ladder. Mal moved up behind him. She could see the second rugger was on its side nearby.

"Stay in the vehicle." Rhain stood on the roof.

"If we hit another mine, we'll be blown into tiny pieces," Thadd said. "The shield won't take another blast."

Mal's gut cramped. She was hating this Krastin more and more.

Rhain lifted his hand and closed his eyes. Energy filled the air and she felt it pool around her, She wasn't staying down here. Not if she could help.

She climbed up the ladder and moved up beside him on the roof.

Ahead of the rugger, she saw the dirt shiver, and an object flew up out of the ground. Rhain moved his fingers, and the object crushed into a tiny ball of crumpled metal.

Oh, God. He was pulling the mines up. More of them wiggled out of the ground.

She watched him grit his teeth. Multiple mines shot up; they were twisted things covered in spikes, and he destroyed all of them before they dropped harmlessly back to the ground.

"Can't... Keep this up much longer," he said between gritted teeth.

Led by some unknown instinct, Mal moved closer and pressed her hands to his arm.

He opened his silver eyes and looked at her, his irises glowing.

The energy in her uncoiled and flowed into him. She gasped. It didn't hurt, but it felt strange.

His eyes flared.

All around them, mines flew up, high into the air. They crunched and twisted into nothingness.

"It's clear," he said, his voice strained. "Let's get the other rugger upright, and get to Emex." He met her gaze. "Thank you, Mal."

BACK IN THE RUGGER, tremors of energy still rippled through Rhain's system.

Somehow, Mal had *passed* energy into him.

It was impossible.

No Zhalton could do that. They could draw from the field, charge objects and machines, but not pass energy between people. There were always those who attempted it, but none had ever succeeded. The closest they had to it was what healers like Tavith could do.

He eyed her, sitting quietly beside him.

She opened her eyes. "All right, spit it out."

"Spit?" He frowned.

"It's a phrase. Say whatever is bothering you."

"What you did, giving me energy, Zhaltons can't do that."

Her mouth opened. "Oh."

"Oh, is right."

"I just wanted to help and did what felt natural."

"You did help." He grabbed her hand. "Mal, what you did... It's special."

Her cheeks colored. "I'm not doing anything special. Rhain, I'm stumbling around in the dark with these new abilities."

He squeezed her hand. "I'm here. I'll help you any way I can."

"Thanks," she murmured.

"Rhain?" Thadd's voice. It was tense.

Rhain rose and walked to the front cabin. "What is it?"

"Overlord." The co-driver turned in her seat. "We're picking up strange readings on scanners."

"What kind of readings?"

"We don't know. There are several energy signatures closing in on us."

He looked down at the projection and saw three dots.

"Visual?"

Thadd shook his head. "We can't see anything."

Rhain stooped to look out the window. "But we should be in visual range."

"Yes," Thadd said.

He didn't see anything. They were right at the edge of The Barrens and all he saw was rough, rocky ground.

There were no vehicles in sight.

"Rhain?" Mal stood behind him. His first instinct was to tell her not to worry. He realized he didn't have to hold back with her. In previous relationships, he'd shielded women from the hard aspects of ruling.

They'd wanted the enjoyment and luxury of being with the king, but not the hardship of difficult times and problematic decisions.

"Three signatures closing in on us."

She looked up. "I don't see anything."

"Nor do I."

"Are they cloaked?"

"Perhaps. Sarkan specializes in weaponry of war."

"They're almost on us," Thadd said.

Rhain looked out at the other rugger.

Suddenly, something speared up out of the ground, rocks and dirt flying into the air.

"Watch out!" Thadd roared.

Their rugger swerved, and Rhain gripped Mal and the wall to keep them upright.

The second rugger slammed on the brakes. The creature that had erupted from the ground, whipped around and fired on the rugger.

"Shields up!" Rhain roared.

A glimmer of energy moved over their vehicle. He hoped the shields had recharged enough.

The other rugger took a hit, shaking violently. Its shield shimmered to life.

"Open fire," Rhain ordered.

The drivers fired on the vehicle. Rhain realized then that it wasn't a creature. Not fully.

It had tracks for legs and feet, and a pointed front end for digging through the ground. It had a taller back end, and some organic armor in parts.

A Zhylaw creation.

The rugger shot short pulses of energy at the Zhylaw vehicle.

They clipped it, but it sped off.

"The other rugger is having engine problems," Thadd said.

"We need to keep the Zhylaw off them," Rhain barked.

He raced back inside the rugger and popped open the top hatch again.

"Rhain—" Thadd sounded ready to complain.

"It'll be fine, Thadd. Keep firing on them. Activate the turrets if required."

Mal watched him, worry in her eyes.

"Stay," he said. "I'll be back."

He climbed out of the hatch and watched as another Zhylaw vehicle burst up through the dirt.

The vehicles converged on the struggling rugger. His rugger fired, sending them scattering.

Rhain concentrated on one of the Zhylaw vehicles. He focused his power. He was tired from clearing the mines, so it felt sluggish.

The Zhylaw vehicle sped up, about to ram the stricken rugger—

His energy wrapped around it. It stopped, like it hit a wall. It lifted off the ground and he heard its engine straining.

He curled his fingers together.

The vehicle started to crumple in on itself and then there was a vicious crunch, and he jerked his arm, flinging the destroyed vehicle away.

Cheers erupted from his people.

Rhain was spent. He'd used too much energy, too fast.

He heard a whirring sound and turned. Two turrets rose up on the back of his rugger. Thadd sat in one, his rugged face set like stone.

Mal sat in the other.

The turrets swiveled, and they opened fire on the Zhylaw.

The two remaining Zhylaw vehicles dodged and weaved.

Rhain looked at the struggling rugger. It still wasn't operational, and he heard the whine of its engine as they tried to get it started.

Thadd and Mal fired shots of energy, trying to keep the Zhylaw off the rugger.

Rhain yelled down at the drivers. "Get as close to the other rugger as you can."

"Yes, Overlord."

They gunned across the rocky ground.

"Keep them busy," he yelled at Mal and Thadd.

They got close to the rugger. Rhain rose up, then leaped onto the other vehicle.

A head popped up through the hatch, weapon in hand.

The fighter's eyebrows rose. "Overlord."

"Hang on."

He opened a panel on the top of the rugger and thrust his palm against the engine. He pushed the last of his power into it.

It hurt, because he had to pull from so deep within himself.

The engine turned over.

"Get moving and get to Emex," he ordered.

"Yes, sir." The man disappeared back inside.

As the second rugger passed by, Rhain leaped back across. He almost fell, his legs like water. He'd overtaxed himself and had no energy left. He went down on one knee.

"Rhain!"

He looked up at Mal in the turret seat. "I'm fine."

She paused to swivel and fire. Ahead, the other rugger shot off toward the outpost.

They followed, bumping over the rough ground.

"Overlord!" Shouts from inside the rugger.

"Yes."

"We have more Zhylaw signatures incoming."

Rhain's gut knotted. The other two were still chasing them.

"How many?"

"Seven."

Gorr.

They couldn't fight that many. "We have to get to Emex." He looked up at Mal and Thadd. "We have to keep them off us and get to the outpost."

Their rugger sped up. He gripped a metal handhold to hold himself in place. The wind whipped at his hair.

Mal and Thadd laid down continuous fire.

Rhain turned his head and spotted the outpost ahead.

It was centered on a large hill, and ringed by a solid metal wall. The blue energy shield glimmered over it.

They'd be safe inside.

He turned back and saw Mal hit a Zhylaw vehicle with a burst of energy. It swerved, hit a rock, and went airborne. It crashed back down and rolled.

Yes. Rhain smiled.

Then behind them, the ground started to shake.

Another Zhylaw vehicle broke through the surface.

His chest locked. Then another. And another.

More vehicles came to the surface, and they all sped after them.

"Oh, fuck." Mal fired wildly.

"Keep them off us." Rhain looked down into the open hatch. "I need an energy bomb."

A fighter handed him one of the small, round devices.

He held it in his palm and charged it. It hurt. The energy ripped out of his very core, and he bowed his head and gritted his teeth. Lights blinked on over the surface of the ball, then he drew his arm back and tossed it. It rolled into the incoming Zhylaw vehicles.

It exploded.

One vehicle went airborne, and crashed down on another. Another swerved and slowed.

"Emex is opening the gates," the driver called from inside.

Rhain swiveled. He saw the first rugger race inside the outpost.

Come on. He urged the driver to go faster.

The Zhylaw were almost on them.

A second later, their rugger tore into the outpost. The door shimmered back in place and a Zhylaw vehicle hit it, exploding into pieces.

Cheers went up, and the rugger screeched to a stop.

Rhain met Mal's gaze. She grinned, and he grinned back.

Then Rhain collapsed.

"I'M FINE, THADD."

Rhain's captain hovered near him, glowering. The Emex Outpost medica stepped back, the green energy on her hands dimming.

"The overlord is perfectly fine," the woman said with a smile. "He just over-taxed himself. A good night of rest will be the best medicine."

Mal stood by the wall, worry lining her face.

Rhain opened his arms, and when she hurried over and stepped into them, he felt better already.

Thadd eyed them, while the medica pretended to be busy with some work.

Rhain kissed her temple. "I'm fine."

"You sure?" Mal murmured.

He stroked her back. "Positive." He tipped her face up. "I need to meet with Aran, the head of the outpost. Go with Thadd. I'll come and find you when I'm finished."

She nodded and stepped back. After she and Thadd left, Aran entered.

Power emanated off the young man. He was the heir to a powerful House that possessed strong abilities, and the son of the Duke of Davix.

The medica nodded. "I'll see to the rest of the injured."

Rhain rose and held a palm out. Aran touched his to Rhain's and a faint pulse of energy exchanged between them.

"Good to see you up, Overlord."

"Thank you, Aran. How's the shield?"

"At full strength." The outpost leader led Rhain out into the hall. "No Zhylaw will be getting through."

Aran led them down some stairs and then out onto a balcony. Down below, mining processing equipment hummed and chugged.

"We're running at close to capacity, but we had to shut down some outlying mining posts outside the shield, Overlord. The hexid attacks have been increasing."

Rhain watched several mining staff members monitoring the equipment. He saw the lights on the side of the machines, and felt the hum of energy off them.

"You're doing a great job here, Aran." Rhain turned to look out at the landscape—the rocky nightmare toward the Badus Mountains in one direction, and the green fields back toward Citadel in the other.

Sometimes it was how Rhain felt inside—dark and light in constant battle.

"Overlord, our scanners detect large numbers of hexids and Zhylaw vehicles. They're staying hidden, but they're waiting for you to reemerge from the shield."

"I know," Rhain said grimly.

Krastin had them trapped.

For now.

Several of Rhain's fighters were injured from the journey to the outpost. They needed the night to heal before they could move.

He felt an ache inside him, and realized that he missed Mal. He didn't like her being out of sight. He'd known her such a short time, but she was becoming vitally important to him.

His. He wanted her to be his. Wanted her trust, her loyalty, and....

Well, there were emotions Rhain hadn't considered yet.

He'd always believed that he was too driven by his duty to feel. But one tough woman from Earth was proving him wrong.

He turned to Aran. "We'll wait for your medica to heal my fighters. Continue to monitor the Zhylaw. And I need you to find a way out of here for me."

Aran nodded. "Consider it done, my lord. We've prepared quarters for you all. Not quite as comfortable as

Citadel, but I've earmarked our garden, the Lindera, for your personal use."

Rhain clasped the man's shoulder. "Thank you again, Aran."

"Of course, Overlord."

Rhain went looking for Mal. He headed down to the lower level, and heard noises coming from the training courtyard. The very familiar sounds of fighting.

He turned a corner and froze.

Mal was facing off with Thadd.

They both ignored the available weapons and were fighting hand-to-hand. Thadd wore no armor, just a bare chest, leathers, and a harness.

His captain was built of slabs of muscle, and he outweighed Mal by a large amount.

Rhain tensed. This fight was not equally balanced. One wrong move and Thadd could hurt her.

The pair rushed at each other. Mal used her smaller size and speed to her advantage. She ducked low, then landed a quick kick to Thadd's leg.

Rhain's captain grunted and spun. He tried to catch her, but she was gone.

They circled each other, and this time, Thadd lunged.

Mal planted her legs, bent her knees, and grabbed Thadd.

The next thing Rhain knew, Thadd's big body flew over Mal, and he crashed to the floor.

Thadd growled and leaped to his feet. "What was that?"

"A little judo throw. It's a type of fighting style on Earth."

"I want to learn it."

"I'll think about teaching it to you."

Thadd's gaze narrowed on her.

Mal rushed at him. They traded kicks and hits, moving across the training space. Thadd was power and strength, and Mal was grit and smarts.

Thadd swung, but Mal miscalculated. The blow caught her midsection and lifted her off her feet.

She flew through the air and slammed down on her back.

Rhain saw red.

He didn't think, couldn't. He charged across the training yard and slammed into Thadd.

His friend grunted. With a shoulder in the man's gut, Rhain lifted him off his feet and slammed him against the wall.

"Rhain—" Thadd wheezed between gritted teeth.

"You don't hurt her. *Ever*."

"I didn't...mean..."

"Rhain." Mal's voice.

He felt a touch on his arm, her hand sliding down to his wrist.

He realized his energy had flared and was whipping around him. His chest heaved.

She leaned into him. "I'm fine. I asked Thadd to spar with me. I don't mind knocking him around, and he doesn't go easy on me."

Rhain tensed. Thadd stayed calm, watching his face.

"He's bigger and stronger than you," Rhain bit out.

"I can take care of myself. Rhain, he's your best friend and bodyguard, he wasn't going to hurt me."

Rational thought started to seep into his brain. It was far easier when she was pressed against his side. He released Thadd and stepped back.

"Thadd—"

"It's fine, Rhain." He looked between Rhain and Mal. "I get it." Thadd stepped forward. "I saw the way she helped you on the journey here. She fought beside you every step of the way. I'll protect her with my life, as I do you." He bowed his head.

Rhain blew out a breath. "I know that."

With a nod, Thadd walked away.

Mal stepped in front of Rhain and cupped his cheeks.

"Hey." Her fingers stroked his stubbled cheeks. "And I thought I was tense."

"I dislike feeling trapped, and I hate seeing you hurt."

"A few bumps and bruises don't count. I'm fine." She went up on her toes and kissed his nose.

The scent of her filled him, and he pulled her closer. She hugged him back.

"I hate not being able to go out there right now," she said.

"I know."

"All I can think about is poor Poppy." Mal stepped back. She rubbed the center of her chest with her knuckles. "It's like a pull, a hollow ache. A compulsion."

And it hurt her not to follow it.

"Tonight, my fighters need time to heal," he said. "We'll rest so we can be ready to face the Barrens, and find Poppy."

"And Krastin."

"And Krastin," he agreed.

Rhain knew they needed to put the tension aside, or they'd never get any sleep.

"Come with me." He took her hand and led her inside.

"Where are you taking me?"

"I want to show you something."

He led her through the maze of corridors of the outpost. It was starker and more industrial than the palace. It was clear that this was a working outpost, not a vacation spot.

They passed some mine workers, who bowed their heads at Rhain. He led her up some stairs.

"Man, you Zhaltons love stairs."

He smiled at her and reached a doorway. He pressed a palm to it and it shimmered open.

Her jaw dropped. "Oh, wow."

It was the Lindera. The garden was filled with plants that grew thick and green. One side was food plants for the outpost, but the rest was flowers for various uses.

They passed under a vine laden with white rillis. As they passed another bush, flowers unfurled, sensing their presence. They were pretty, yellow bells.

"These are nerine, also called welcome bells." He reached over to another plant and plucked a blue, trumpet-shaped bloom off a vine. He brushed it over her cheek and lips.

"I feel the energy off it," she said.

"Yes. Allium flowers are full of energy." He tucked it behind her ear. They followed the path through the garden. The sky overhead was just starting to ignite with auroras.

A pool appeared—it was oval-shaped and lined with flat rocks.

Mal gasped.

"What?" he asked.

"I saw this place. In the vision with the energy witch."

"And?"

She turned to him. "We were both naked."

His lips quirked, his body instantly responding to her words. "*Really*?"

CHAPTER THIRTEEN

Mal kicked off her boots. The grass was cool and lush under her feet.

The garden had an almost magical feel. She sensed pops of energy from the flowers.

She turned to Rhain. He stood there—big, larger than life. He was so rugged and masculine, with power throbbing off him. His eyes were more gray than silver right now, and his face looked fierce.

"Mine," he said, his voice low and gritty.

"No, I belong to me," she countered.

He stepped closer to her. "You can also belong to me."

She shivered. "Am I just a novelty to you? You have a palace full of soft, beautiful women."

"I don't want them. I want you. I want to protect you, have you by my side."

So many emotions curled inside her. She wasn't sure how she felt exactly, or where this was headed, but she knew she wanted him.

She shimmied out of her pants and unwound her top.

His gaze narrowed on her, like a raptor. She stood naked, then walked toward him.

His hands curled into fists at his sides. She pressed her palms to his chest. One of his hands snaked up and slid into her hair. Hard enough that she felt the tug.

"You make me want things, Mal. Make me want to do all kinds of things to you."

Her pulse sped up, and she was damp between her thighs. "So do them. For one night, I want to forget. I just want it to be me and you."

He kissed her. Then he lifted her off her feet and carried her toward the edge of the pool.

She kissed him back, desperately, hungrily. Then he laid her on the grass, and it was soft like a blanket beneath her.

He stood above her and shed his clothes.

Her chest hitched. He was so damn magnificent. She wanted to bite him all over.

He unbuckled his harness and dropped it onto the grass nearby. Now, she licked her lips and pressed her thighs together. His large, erect cock rose up, and she couldn't take her gaze off it.

Rhain knelt and pushed her legs apart. He was breathing harshly.

"Come inside me, Rhain. I need you inside me."

He lunged forward, covering her with his body. She felt his energy splay out around him, and her own rose to meet his. It electrified her skin.

Rhain slid an arm under her hips, yanking her up.

"*Yes*," she breathed.

He grabbed his cock, then guided it to her.

Mal bit her lip. Her gaze met his.

He thrust inside her.

She'd taken him before, but it felt like the first time all over again. Her body stretched to accommodate his thick invasion.

But Rhain's patience was gone.

He began thrusting into her heavily, every plunge deep. She raked her nails down his biceps, crying out.

"Mallory," he groaned.

"*Rhain!*"

The angle of his thrusts brushed her clit. She cried out.

He threw his head back, the muscles in his neck straining. Mal absorbed every sound he made, the heavy thrust of his hips, the deep stretch of his cock inside her.

Her release hit, splintering her apart.

She clung to him, her anchor, her rock in the storm. Waves of pleasure crashed over her.

He made a tortured sound, and with one last thrust, poured himself inside her.

Finally, he shifted, collapsing partly to the side but still inside her. He kept her pinned to him, his breathing harsh.

"That was..." She couldn't find a word adequate enough.

"It was." His voice was low and hoarse.

They held onto each other as their skin cooled. It was really scary how right this felt. She rubbed her cheek against his shoulder. How for the first time in her life, she understood what it felt like to know you were in the right place.

She just wasn't sure Rhain felt the same way. And if he did, how long it would last.

Stop thinking, Mal.

She ran a hand up his sweat slicked back. "I guess we could have a swim in the pool."

"We could." He moved his hips.

Mal gasped. *God.* He was still thick and hard inside her.

"Or, I have a better idea," he said.

He rolled onto his back, keeping her in place. She rose above him, straddling him, his cock deep inside her.

Mal rocked her hips. "I do like your idea."

THE NEXT MORNING, Rhain strode into the front courtyard of the outpost.

The pleasures of the night before seemed very far away. He was dressed in his armor, swords on his back.

It was time to head out and find Krastin.

"Overlord." Aran hurried over. "I hope you slept well."

He'd slept with his face buried in Mal's silky hair. "I did."

"My team had an excellent idea for how you can get out."

Rhain looked up and saw Thadd and the other fighters gathered. Everyone looked prepared.

His captain nodded.

"You go out in our mining transports," Aran said. "They're not as fast as your ruggers, but they're sturdy and built for the terrain."

Rhain frowned. "Go on."

"I'll have some of my people take your ruggers, and lead the Zhylaw away."

"And we sneak out while they're busy." Thadd pointed. "I took the liberty of transferring some extra weapons to the mining ruggers."

The mining ruggers were built of a dark-black metal, and rode lower to the ground, with a small flat bed at the back, no doubt for transporting equipment and craxma metal.

Rhain looked at Aran. "It's a good idea, Aran. But I don't want your people hurt."

The man nodded. "They won't be. They know this terrain well. They'll get back inside the shield once you're clear."

Mal strode out of the nearby building.

She wore Zhalton armor, and the bronze metal hugged her trim torso, leather trousers slicking down her legs. Her sword hung in a scabbard on her back. Her hair was in a tight ponytail that bobbed as she walked.

Her face was resolute, composed. She was ready for battle.

In his head, he had a flash of her naked and under him, taking him.

His gut clenched.

Mal was his. He'd keep her safe, then he just had to

finally convince her to trust him. Convince her that she belonged here with him.

"Ready?" she asked.

Rhain told her the plan.

She smiled. "I like it. Simple but sneaky."

"The mining ruggers are almost ready to go," Thadd said.

Mal swiveled and rubbed her fist against her chest. "The tug feels stronger today."

Rhain gripped her shoulder. "We're going to find her."

Mal nodded.

Soon, they were loading into the mining ruggers. It was a tighter fit, and not as comfortable as the ones they'd arrived in. Thadd had set up turrets in the beds on the back. The captain sat in the seat of one, and another fighter, Lira, sat on the turret on the second mining rugger.

Inside the vehicle, Rhain sat behind the drivers, Mal beside him.

They listened to Aran on the comm line.

"Open the shield. Send out the decoys."

Rhain leaned forward, tense, and he watched as the ruggers they'd arrived in from Citadel zoomed out the front gate of Emex Outpost. Aran's mechanics had worked all night to fix most of the damage the ruggers had received the day before.

There were only two people in each—Aran's best drivers who knew the terrain around Emex best.

"Pull up the projection," Rhain ordered.

They watched a bird's-eye view from the Emex cameras. The two ruggers spread out, driving hard and fast. At first, nothing happened. They raced across the terrain.

"Where are they?" Mal muttered.

"*There*," Rhain pointed.

Two Zhylaw vehicles burst out of the ground in pursuit.

Mal sucked in a breath.

Another appeared. And another one right in front of the ruggers. The ruggers swerved.

The two vehicles raced on, taking a wild, zigzagging path across the countryside.

"It's clear." Aran appeared outside their mining rugger and banged his palm on the side of it. "Go now."

"Move out," Rhain ordered.

Their rugger went first. They exited the outpost and turned away to the north, away from the other ruggers. They would take a more circuitous path to avoid detection.

They bumped over the rocky ground. It was a much rougher ride than the regular transport ruggers.

"Anything on scans?" Mal asked.

"Nothing," the driver, Cedo, responded.

All the fighters in the vehicle sat silent, tense.

"Overlord," the co-driver, Kasra, said. "Emex just sent a message. The ruggers returned safely."

Rhain blew out a breath, and he saw Mal smile.

"Excellent," he said.

Now they just had to reach their destination safely.

They moved further north before slowly veering to the east. He saw Mal rubbing her chest again.

"Are you okay?" he asked.

She nodded.

He took her hand. He felt the interested gazes of his fighters but ignored them.

"It feels stronger," she said.

"Because we're getting closer."

There was a thump on the roof of the vehicle. "Rhain?" Thadd's deep voice. "You'd better get up here."

Rhain frowned and opened the top hatch. He popped his head up. Mal squeezed up beside him.

Ahead, in the distance, a thick, black cloud lay ahead of them, filling the horizon.

"What is that?" Mal breathed.

"I don't know," Rhain ducked down. "Cedo, scan the fog."

"There's nothing on scans. It's not noxious, but the scans can't penetrate it."

Rhain scowled. He didn't like this.

"If we try to go around it, it'll take too long," Mal said.

There were no good choices.

"Fighters, secure your harnesses," Rhain said. "We are heading into the black fog."

They all waited, tense as they drove on. A few faint wisps of fog crept around the vehicles, hanging in the air. It wasn't too thick yet, but they were right at the edge of it. It looked like smoke.

Tension gripped everyone.

Beep.

Rhain looked at the drivers.

Kasra cursed. "Contact. We have a Zhylaw signature inbound and moving fast."

"Thadd!" Rhain roared.

"I'm ready," Thadd yelled back.

Mal's hands flexed, like she wanted to draw her sword.

"Second quadrant," Cedo yelled.

Rhain swiveled and looked out the narrow window. A Zhylaw vehicle burst through the ground.

In the turret, Thadd swiveled and fired.

Energy pulses lit up the thickening fog. The second rugger fired on the Zhylaw vehicle as well. Then, another Zhylaw vehicle streamed up out of the ground.

Thadd kept firing.

The Zhylaw vehicle hit a rock, tipped over, and crashed on its side.

They continued firing on it.

Screams cut through the air and Rhain popped his head up through the hatch.

He saw the shadows of several hexids leap onto the second rugger.

One grabbed Lira out of the turret seat and tossed her on the ground.

No. "Bring us around. Thadd, Lira is down!"

"I see her." Thadd fired.

Rhain climbed on the roof and knelt. He lifted his palm. After a night of rest, his energy was fully charged.

The hexid raised its claws, about to slash the struggling Lira. He let loose with a red pulse.

The hexid flew back.

"Thadd, get Lira and join the other rugger. I'll cover you."

His captain of the guard didn't hesitate. He leaped off and sprinted toward the fallen woman.

Rhain jumped in the turret and fired on the hexids. Mal appeared and knelt on the roof.

"Get back inside."

"No." She drew her sword.

He ground his teeth together, then saw Thadd scoop up the now-unconscious Lira.

Rhain fired on the hexids until Thadd leaped high in the air, and landed on top of the other rugger.

Rhain expelled a breath and watched as his captain handed Lira down into the rugger. Then he leaped onto the abandoned turret.

"Let's go!" Rhain yelled.

Their rugger followed the second one, and they drove deeper into the fog. It got thicker and darker with each passing moment. Visibility was terrible.

"This is all Krastin's doing," Rhain said.

The ruggers slowed. It was too dangerous to go any faster. He stared into the black. Were those shadows?

Then Mal made a sound. "Where did the other rugger go?"

Rhain scanned the fog. There was no sign of Thadd's vehicle. "I don't see them. I can't see anything."

"Overlord, we've lost contact with the others," Kasra called out. "The fog is blocking communication."

Mal cursed.

"Wait." Kasra appeared at the hatch, looking up at

them. "I'm detecting a signature." The woman's voice was strained. "A *very* large signature in the fog. "

"What is it?" Rhain asked.

"I don't know, my lord. But it's big."

Rhain looked at Mal. She lifted her sword and stared into the fog.

CHAPTER FOURTEEN

Mal's heart was hammering hard.

Shit, she hated this fog. It was dense and black like smoke.

She couldn't see the other rugger anywhere. The gnawing ache was still chewing on her chest.

"Come on." She'd take pretty much anything over this waiting and not knowing what was out there.

She felt a vibration.

She glanced at Rhain. His brows were drawn as he stared into the fog.

More vibrations.

Something was coming.

The fog cleared a little.

Then a giant leg slammed down in front of them.

Her heart jumped into her throat. *What the hell?* She looked up. The creature was *huge.*

More of the colossal beast appeared out of the fog, and she could do nothing more than stare.

Behind her, Rhain cursed.

Yeah, the universe really had it out for her.

The creature looked similar to a hexid, except it was absolutely towering. It no longer walked upright, and instead walked on all fours, had a huge tail, and an armored head.

"Have you seen this guy before?" she asked.

"No."

How had Krastin even gotten it here?

The giant creature gave a roar. The sound blasted through Mal's bones. She tightened her grip on her sword.

The beast lifted a foot and started to slam it down.

"Go! *Go!*" Rhain yelled.

The rugger tore off. Mal gripped a hand hold on the roof so she wouldn't be thrown off.

They drove right under the enormous creature. It frantically stomped the ground, trying to find them.

"If we can disable the legs, it can't move," she said.

Rhain nodded and swiveled the turret. He opened fire on the closest leg.

The noise the giant hexid made was deafening.

Mal leaned back and poked her head down into the rugger. "Let's go. We need to target the legs."

The other fighters clambered out of the rugger.

Mal leaped onto the ground, the fighters landing beside her.

She looked back at Rhain, and their gazes met.

Be safe. She charged her weapon and it glowed in the fog. It was easier to do now. The other fighters charged their weapons, and the glow of energy lit up the dark fog around them.

"Let's do this," she cried.

Mal ran forward. She raced toward the massive back leg of the beast and lifted her sword. She swiped and cut into the tough, leathery flesh, but it barely reacted.

It was like poking a giant with a pin.

She sliced again. *Shit.* Did it even feel that?

Rhain kept firing the turret. Energy blasts hit the giant hexid's head and it roared.

"Everyone, target this leg," she yelled at the fighters.

Two stood back, firing crossbows. The charged bolts hit the creature and flesh exploded.

Mal sliced again. Next to her, Carvia sliced with her sword and Trist with a small axe. Together, they cut and hacked. Chunks of putrid flesh fell off.

The hexid stopped, and swiped its front leg out. It kicked rocks into the air.

"Watch out!" Mal dodged.

A rock skimmed over her head.

The giant hexid turned and she cut into its leg again. Everything was slick with blood and she dug her blade in deep. She could see muscles and tendons. She had to keep cutting.

The creature shifted its feet and the fighters all leaped out of the way.

Suddenly, she heard shouts.

Mal spun and saw the giant tail whipping right at her. It slammed into her, knocking her off her feet.

She hit the ground hard and rolled. Pain clamped on her ribs and her head swam. Her gaze turned murky, and she fought through the agony. She dragged in a breath.

Fuck, it hurt. So much.

She bit her tongue and tasted blood.

Carvia ran up to her, shouting something, but Mal's ears were ringing. The woman held out her hand.

Get up, Mal.

She took Carvia's hand and the fighter hauled Mal upright. Then she yanked Mal forward and she stumbled behind the woman.

The colossal hexid's foot crashed down, right where she'd been lying.

She looked up and saw the creature stomping again. Rhain was still firing from the turret. The creature zeroed in on the rugger.

Oh, God. Mal's heart jumped into her throat. "Get off there!"

Rhain kept firing.

Trist darted in, tossing several knives at the hexid's injured leg.

The creature bellowed and shifted. Trist dodged...the wrong way.

"No!" Carvia screamed.

The creature's foot slammed down on the man.

Mal's gut curdled. *No, no, no.*

She couldn't look at the remains of poor Trist. All she could do was focus on bringing the beast down.

Carvia was frozen, her face twisted in shock and grief.

"Not now, Carvia," Mal shouted. "Focus on the back leg."

The tail swung again and Mal shoved the swordswoman out of the way, then ducked.

Dammit. They were going to die here if they didn't bring the damn thing down.

Suddenly, a big body sprinted in front of them, right under the hexid.

Rhain raised his arms, and she saw him grit his teeth. Energy pulsed through the fog—strong and potent.

The colossal hexid froze. It roared, unable to move.

"Do it!" he cried, voice hoarse.

"Come on," Mal yelled. "For Trist."

They sprinted to the leg. She raised her sword and stabbed deep.

They needed to cut enough vital things so that it couldn't move. The others were with her. *Stab. Stab. Slice.*

She hit something and black blood sprayed over them all. *Ugh.*

Face a terrible mask, Carvia slashed wildly.

The creature's leg started to collapse.

"Watch out," someone yelled.

The huge body came crashing down. Mal ran and slammed into Rhain.

"Okay?" He cupped her cheek.

She felt like she'd been hit by a sledgehammer and her ribs ached, but she nodded.

"Trist..." she said.

Rhain's face twisted. "I saw."

"Watch out for that tail!" Another fighter yelled.

The tail was still moving. The creature let out an enraged sound and the tail whipped around, like a giant battering ram.

It crashed into their rugger.

The rugger went airborne, hit the ground, and rolled over and over.

"*Gorr!*" Rhain raced toward it.

When he got close, the two drivers climbed out. Mal released a breath. They were alive.

"It's coming back again," Cedo yelled.

Mal whipped around and saw the tail swinging again.

She jerked her hands up. The tail froze and the beast moaned.

She planted her feet and pushed out with all the energy she could muster. Her body hurt and she felt energy flow through her. She concentrated hard. For Trist.

The tail exploded. The colossal hexid roared in pain.

Rhain appeared beside her. He lifted his palm and the damaged rugger lifted into the air. It sailed up to the hexid's huge head. Then the rugger crashed down into its face. Then again. And again.

Mal dropped her hands and touched Rhain's back. She funneled what energy she had left into him. She watched him beat the hexid with the rugger until the vehicle was a misshapen hunk of black metal.

Finally, the hexid collapsed—head bloody and raw.

And very dead.

They were safe.

The energy drained out of Mal and she toppled sideways.

"*Hey.*" Rhain caught her and lowered them both to the ground.

"*Gorr,*" Cedo breathed, staring at the creature.

All the fighters stood by the dead, giant hexid.

"Trist," Carvia said quietly.

"He died with bravery," Rhain said. "A warrior in service to his people."

They were all silent for a moment.

Mal looked around. The creature was dead, but so was one of their own. And their rugger was destroyed. At least the fog had cleared.

She frowned. "Where's the other rugger?"

There was no sign of the vehicle anywhere around them.

RHAIN SCANNED HIS PEOPLE.

Trist was dead, and several were injured. Mal was standing, covered in blood, and he could tell by the way she was holding herself that she was in pain.

He touched her cheek. "Are you all right?"

"I'll live. We need to find the other rugger."

He nodded. "Is everyone okay to walk?"

There were nods and mutters.

"Cedo, grab anything we can salvage from the smashed rugger."

The driver frowned. "I'll see if we can get into it."

It was pretty mangled. As Cedo and Kasra checked the rugger, Rhain slid an arm around Mal.

She leaned into him.

He let his energy slide over her, checking her injuries.

"What are you doing?" Her brow creased.

"Checking that you really are okay."

She wrinkled her nose. "I am. Conserve your energy. I'm guessing we'll need it."

He ruffled her hair. "You did very well against the creature."

She gave him a faint smile. "You too."

"Are you *sure* you aren't hurt?"

"I'm sure I'll have some killer bruises, but I'm upright." She frowned. "I still feel the pull. Toward Poppy."

"We'll find her. Now, let's find the other rugger."

The drivers hadn't been able to salvage much, but soon they all spread out and started walking east.

The fog had gone, like it had never been there to begin with.

Ahead, Carvia broke into a jog and crouched. "I found something."

Rhain took Mal's hand and hurried over.

"Tracks," the fighter said.

They were definitely rugger tire tracks.

"We'll follow them," Rhain said.

The group moved into a jog, following the marks. Suddenly, a figure emerged in the distance.

Rhain frowned. They were too far away to see who it was.

"I got a set of optics from the rugger." Cedo handed the vision device over to Rhain.

In the distance, the figure staggered.

Rhain lifted the optics and zoomed in. "It's Lira."

From the other rugger.

They all picked up speed, but before they reached

her, Lira collapsed. Rhain dropped down beside the woman and turned her over.

There were gasps. She had several black bolts stuck in her chest.

Gorr.

"Herris." The man was their fighter with the best healing abilities.

The tall, bulky Herris knelt. "I'll see what I can do now." He held his palms up and closed his eyes. "She's hurt badly."

"Can we remove the bolts?" Rhain asked.

"Give me a moment. I need to stabilize her."

Rhain heard Mal ordering the others to form a perimeter. They didn't want to get ambushed while busy healing Lira.

"Okay, Overlord," Herris said. "Pull out the first one."

Rhain yanked it out.

Lira reared up, making a hoarse, pained sound.

"*Shh.*" Herris used his energy. "Next one."

It was a slow, laborious process. They couldn't go faster because Lira's body was in shock. After every bolt was removed, Herris had to stabilize her.

Finally, Rhain pulled the last bolt free. Herris kept working on the injured woman.

"I...can't keep going." There was sweat on the man's head, lines bracketing his mouth.

"Mal?" Rhain called out.

She limped over, moving stiffly.

Rhain frowned. She needed to be checked and healed as well.

"Herris is running low on energy. Lira will die without more healing."

Mal swallowed. "Okay." She dragged in a deep breath. "Herris, can I touch your arm?"

The man frowned. "Okay."

"It's fine, Herris. Trust her."

"I'm kind of new at this." Mal placed her palm on the man's bicep.

Rhain felt a strange prick of annoyance. A part of him didn't want her touching another man, but he forced the sensation away. This was life or death.

Mal closed her eyes.

Herris stiffened. "Auroras above," he breathed.

He spread his palms and energy flared on them brightly. It was a deep orange with a touch of green.

Rhain watched Lira's wounds start to knit together.

"She's feeding him energy," someone whispered.

"That's not possible."

"Lira's healed," Herris said, voice tired.

Mal stepped back, swayed.

Rhain slid an arm around her. She was pale but smiling.

All of a sudden, Lira sat up and sucked in a sharp breath.

Rhain squeezed Mal's hand, then crouched beside his healed fighter. "Lira, you're safe."

The woman dragged in a shuddering breath. "Overlord."

"What happened?"

"We were attacked in the fog." She took in a shuddering breath. "Hexids and cupra." She shivered. "We were overrun. The captain kept fighting, to buy us time to escape, but the beasts overwhelmed us. I ran to get help."

"Okay. You're safe now." Rhain looked at Herris. "Can you carry her?"

"I can walk," Lira insisted.

"Herris will help you. Let's find the rest of our team."

They set off, following the tracks again. Everyone was tense, alert.

The Barrens were hot, steam coming off the rocks. A lava pool roiled in the distance.

Mal slowed, looking to the horizon.

"Mal?"

"I...sense something ahead."

Her energy abilities were continuing to grow. He felt a faint tickle of something, but it was still vague.

They kept moving.

Then Rhain made out a twisted shape on the ground.

"The rugger!" someone called out.

Rhain broke into a run.

The vehicle was tipped on its side, dented and beaten up. His pulse pounded. Mal stopped beside him and grabbed his arm.

"Rhain?"

There were several bodies near the vehicle. He ground his teeth together. His people were dead.

Fury and grief twisted inside him.

Thadd. He didn't see Thadd.

"Auroras above," Cedo murmured. "They're all dead."

"They took a lot with them," Carvia gritted out.

There were numerous hexid and cupra corpses

nearby. Rhain circled the rugger. He heard a sound—a rasping hack.

He saw a fighter.

"Zand." Rhain ran and dropped to his knees. The young man was propped up in a sitting position against the wrecked rugger.

Blood stained Zand's chest and mouth. "Overlord." He lifted a shaking hand.

Rhain took it.

"We...fought hard."

"I see that."

"We took down as many as we could."

"You did well, Zand."

"There were so many." He coughed and blood sprayed on his lips.

"Herris!" Rhain called.

The man knelt beside Rhain. "I'm drained, Overlord." Sorrow was thick in his voice.

"I have a little healing ability." Carvia knelt. "Hi, Zand."

"Hi..."

She held her palm over his ripped-up chest.

"Thadd..." Zand coughed again. "The Zhylaw took him."

Rhain stiffened. "What?"

"The Zhylaw warlord took Thadd. The captain fought hard, but they put him in manacles."

Rhain's insides felt frozen.

"I..." Zand squeezed Rhain's hand. "Overlord, I..." The young man slumped.

Carvia sat back. "He's unconscious. I don't know if I can save him."

"Do your best, Carvia."

Rhain rose and stalked away to the edge of the group. He stared blindly at the rocky landscape.

Then he felt a touch on his back. Mal leaned into him.

He closed his eyes and absorbed the feel of her.

"We'll rescue him," she said. "I feel the pull. We're close."

But how could they fight, when they were injured, tired, and bloodied?

She stepped in front of him.

Then he watched the color drain from her face. She started to collapse.

Rhain caught her. "Mal!"

"We have to stop meeting like this." Her voice was a little slurred.

"Take it easy. Don't talk. I've got you."

"I know."

CHAPTER FIFTEEN

"I'm sorry, Overlord," Herris said. "I'm still too spent to heal her."

Mal blinked slowly. She was lying on the ground, her head on Rhain's lap. His face was twisted with frustration.

Her chest throbbed, her ribs ached, and her hip was sore.

"Hey." She grabbed his hand.

He looked at her, then stroked her cheekbone.

"You're injured and you need to rest." He took a deep breath. "We all need time to recuperate."

"Overlord," Kasra said. "There's a rock formation to the east. It sits on higher ground. We can set up a defensive perimeter there."

Rhain nodded. "Let's do it." He lifted Mal into his arms.

"Your Overlordness, I can walk."

"Not today—" his hands tightened on her "—because I'm carrying you."

The hard line of his jaw warned her not to argue. "Fine."

It was a slow walk to the rock pile, with the fighters helping or carrying the injured. The small pile of stones sat on top of the hill.

"Kasra and Cedo, you're on sentry duty," Rhain ordered.

Cedo nodded. "Yes, Overlord."

Rhain set Mal down, leaning her against a large slab of rock.

"I need to check on the others," he said.

She nodded and looked around. Some of the rocks looked like they'd been cut. She frowned and fingered the smooth stone beside her. Was that faint writing engraved on it? It was so weathered that it wasn't clear.

She listened to Rhain talk with his people. Reassuring them, thanking them. That this man thought he was anything like the man that fathered him was crazy.

He finally returned.

"Here." He held out a bottle of water to her.

She sipped it.

He sat beside her. He looked tired, but she knew he'd keep going. He'd never stop.

"Will you call in more fighters?" she asked.

"Comms are blocked." He scowled. "Krastin isn't stupid."

"Hey." She grabbed his arm. "We won't let him win."

Rhain nodded. "I need to check your wounds."

"I'm all right. Herris said he's still tapped out."

"But I'm not."

"Um, Tavith didn't speak very highly of your healing." And she remembered that it hurt him.

"I need you well."

"Rhain—"

He cupped her jaw. "No arguments. I...need this. I need to know that you're okay."

"All right, Rhain." She leaned back.

His face relaxed a little. Carefully, he worked her armor off.

Then he hissed out a breath. "*Mal.*"

Hmm, okay, the bruising was a *little* worse than she'd guessed.

The side of her ribs was already a putrid shade of black. Rhain gently probed, and she hissed out a breath.

"There's nothing broken," she said.

He shot her a hot stare.

Okay, she guessed he didn't care for minor distinctions.

He moved his hands over her and she felt the energy in his palms. It brushed over her skin. The sensation wasn't quite as pleasant as when Tavith healed her. She watched the muscles in Rhain's shoulders tense.

She grabbed his wrist. "It hurts you."

His silver eyes looked molten and alive. "I don't care. I'd take all the hurt from you if I could."

Oh, Rhain. The emotion was clear in his eyes. Knowing that he felt things for her both excited and terrified her. What did she know about loving a man? *Zilch. Nada. Zip.*

She wasn't sure she was built for it. She was pretty

sure she wasn't the kind of woman Rhain's people imagined for him.

But now was not the time to worry about that. They had to rescue Poppy and Thadd.

"There." Rhain sat back.

She felt somewhat better, and the pain had dulled to a low throb. Her bruises were already fading.

Rhain looked so tired.

"Come here," she murmured.

She pulled him down beside her. He leaned against the rock and slid an arm around her.

She leaned into him and let out a breath. Whatever the future held, she had to admit that she felt good right here. With his heartbeat in her ear, feeling safe and protected.

She'd take a moment to enjoy it.

"These rocks look man-made," she said.

He frowned. "They could be. There are some very ancient ruins on the planet. Millennia old. From before the Radiance, and before the first Zhaltons settled here."

"Really?"

"They were left by the Creators."

She turned her head. "Who were the Creators?"

"An advanced species who lived in the galaxy long ago. They seeded life throughout the galaxy. That's why we all look similar, with humanoid features. Our species developed from what the Creators started."

"Hmm. Well, I'm definitely glad we're compatible." She waggled her eyebrows.

He laughed. It was good to hear the sound. "It would be a shame if we weren't." He toyed with her hair.

Around them, the other fighters were resting, eating, and talking quietly. A few were napping, sitting up against the rocks.

Mal heard Rhain pull in a harsh breath.

"You're worried about Thadd?"

"Yes. I know you feel the same way about Poppy."

"I have to believe that she's still alive."

"I'm going to kill Krastin." His tone was hard, resolute.

Fear clutched her. She knew he'd die trying if he had to. She didn't want Rhain to die. She couldn't bear it.

She'd lost everyone she'd ever loved, and she couldn't survive it again.

"So far, Krastin continues to hold the upper hand," Rhain said darkly.

"Not for long." Mal stroked the rock and felt more bumps. "Look. There's some sort of text here."

Rhain leaned forward. "Definitely Creator." He frowned. "I don't recall there being Creator ruins in this area. We've mapped some of the Barrens, but sometimes the lava flows swallow things, and uncover others."

"This looks small." She scanned the rocks. "Like a little outpost."

"Overlord." Carvia appeared. She was doing a bad job of hiding her grief. "Permission for me and Kasra to scout the area."

Rhain frowned. "It's dangerous—"

"We'll stay in visual range, and only search for any sign of the Zhylaw."

He hesitated, then looked toward the setting sun.

"It'll be night soon. We'll have the Barrens beasts to look out for, as well."

"Barrens beasts?" Mal said.

"The native animals, mutated years ago by the Radiance. They've bred over the years and hunt at night."

Mal sighed.

"We won't be long," Carvia said.

It was clear the woman needed to stay busy.

"Go."

Mal watched the pair of fighters jog out, weapons in hand.

Stars started to appear in the sky, and a green aurora flickered to life—bright and lively.

"I want you to stay on Zhalto, Mal."

She froze at Rhain's words.

"After this. You and Poppy can make a home here."

God, she wanted that, too, but her belly was alive with nerves. She hated feeling vulnerable and afraid. What if he changed his mind? What if after a little while, he didn't want her anymore?

She shifted and kissed him. "We'll talk after we rescue Thadd and Poppy," she murmured.

His hands clenched on her, but he nodded.

They rested a little more. Rhain checked on the others. Herris had recovered enough to do some more healing.

"Overlord!" Carvia and Kasra ran back to the camp.

Rhain rose and so did Mal. The pair didn't seem panicked, but more excited.

"My lord, there are huge ruins to the east of here," Kasra said.

"Sprawling Creator ruins," Carvia said.

Mal gasped. "This outpost must've been part of a larger community."

"Where?" Rhain asked.

"There." Carvia pointed.

And in the darkness, Mal saw the glimmer of light.

The fighter straightened. "The Zhylaw are using it as their base."

CHAPTER SIXTEEN

Rhain lay crouched in the darkness, his fighters around him.

They were all still a little battered, but all of them were armed, and ready to follow orders.

Ready to fight.

He held the optics in his hands.

The Creator ruins were carved from the local rock. They were a crumbling mess, almost unrecognizable, except for some walls, pillars, and a few archways dotted through the rocks.

He saw several Zhylaw, and some Sarkan guards. Several hexids sat, crouched on a crumbling rock wall.

They were still, alert.

He passed the optics to Mal and she studied Krastin's base.

"The hexids look like guard dogs, waiting for a target," she said.

Rhain wished he could take her away. Put her somewhere safe. He blew out a breath. She'd never allow that. She'd fight him.

If he put her somewhere safe, she'd crash her way out and rush back into the fight.

He'd fallen in love with a warrior.

His chest tightened. He hadn't truly loved anyone like this before.

He'd always been dedicated to his people, loved his mother, cared deeply for Thadd's family, but he realized he'd held a part of himself back.

Because he came from Zavir.

Because of the pain of losing his mother.

Because no one truly understood how it felt to be king and live for others.

But this woman from Earth had cracked him wide open.

"I feel the pull to that place. Poppy is in there." Mal's face twisted. "There are too many fighters and hexids."

"We'll need to sneak in."

Carvia crouched beside them. "I suggest that some of us cause a diversion. Attack from the front of the ruins and draw out the bulk of Krastin's forces."

Mal grinned. "While a small team sneaks in the back. We'll rescue Thadd and Poppy, and cut off the head of the snake."

Rhain again wanted to tell her to stay here, but he locked it down. "Carvia, you're in charge of the diversion. Herris and Zand, you're with Mal and me."

The two men nodded.

"I have a stash of energy bombs." One of the fighters held up a bag.

"Perfect." Carvia's teeth were white in the darkness. "Trist liked a good bomb. Let's do this for him, and light up the night."

Soon Rhain found himself sneaking closer to the ruins, Mal one step behind him, and Herris and Zand close by.

They moved stealthily, silently. The ruins loomed over them.

He spotted movement in the dark and held up a hand. The others froze.

He saw two hexids run along the wall.

"We wait here," Rhain whispered.

Now they just had to wait for Carvia's team.

He felt the tension pumping off Mal. She knew her friend was close. Rhain hoped Thadd was all right.

Krastin had only taken him to bait Rhain.

Hold on, Thadd. I'm coming. And Krastin will pay.

Suddenly, an explosion rocked the night.

Then another.

Energy filled the air.

Carvia and her team had attacked. Shouts cut through the darkness. The hexids on the wall dashed off.

"Clear," Rhain said. "Let's move."

He moved forward. They picked their way over the rocks. He leaped onto a wall and landed in a crouch. The others followed.

There was a bright glow ahead, deeper into the ruins.

As they approached, he heard a low groan. The hairs on his arms raised. That was Thadd.

They crept forward, and Rhain paused and looked down.

The ruins moved deeper into a natural rock bowl. Mal sucked in a breath. Herris muttered a near-silent curse.

There were creatures in cages. Mostly hexids, but a few others. Some were native Zhalton animals that had been desecrated by the Zhylaw.

Several hexids slammed against the bars—wild and aggressive.

Zhylaw in black uniforms walked between the cages. Some were studying projections, and others held pieces of tech.

There were several benches laid out. Most had animals or people strapped to them.

Rhain's gut curdled.

He heard that deep groan again.

He turned his head and ground his teeth together. Thadd was strapped down to a bench. A Zhylaw scientist poked into his chest, which was cracked open.

Thadd had an implant embedded at his temple, and he thrashed against his bindings.

"I see our latest subject is being stubborn," a sharp voice said.

Krastin stepped into view.

Rhain hadn't realized he'd started to move until Mal grabbed his arm.

"Wait," she whispered urgently.

He saw anger burning in her gaze, and he blew out a breath.

"He is very strong-willed," the scientist said.

"Good. I like breaking strong wills. They make very loyal followers after." Krastin smiled.

"I'll *kill* him," Rhain whispered.

"And I'll help you. But first, we need a plan."

"Can you see Poppy?"

Mal shook her head and bit her lip.

"There's fighting at the entrance, Krastin," someone said.

"The guards will handle it." Krastin's smile turned icy cold. "Overlord Sarkany cannot win this fight. He will die tonight trying to save his man."

"His father wants him alive," the scientist said nervously.

Krastin lifted one shoulder. "And how is our very special test subject?"

"I'm not sure she'll survive the transition, but she's still alive."

"I wish we had access to our full facilities. I hate having to make do." Krastin cast an unhappy look around the ruins.

Then the warlord's gaze swiveled and lifted. Rhain followed it and felt Mal go rigid.

A cage hung from an archway. It was partly blocked by a pillar, so they hadn't noticed it before.

A small, blonde woman lay on the floor of it. Unmoving.

"Poppy," Mal whispered.

Rhain saw the woman jerk, like she was having a seizure.

"She's alive," he said. "We'll get her out."

"What's the plan, Overlord?" Herris asked from behind him.

Rhain studied the area. The hexids were caged, and the scientists were unlikely to be too much of a danger.

"Our priority is freeing Thadd and Poppy." Rhain turned to his fighters. "I'll confront Krastin—"

"Rhain, no." Mal grabbed his hand.

"He's the most dangerous. I'll keep him busy. Mal, you free Thadd. Herris and Zand, find a way to lower Poppy's cage and get her out."

Mal looked away, her lips pressed into a flat line.

Rhain pressed a finger under her chin. "It will be fine. We have to save our friends."

"I worry what risks you'll take to beat Krastin."

He pulled her closer. "Mal—"

She yanked him close and kissed him. "Stay alive, Rhain. We have a conversation to have, remember?"

Love flared inside him. "Stay safe, Mal."

"You too, your Overlordness, or I *will* find a way to make you very sorry."

He believed her. He dropped another kiss to her mouth, then rose. Silently, he moved away from Mal and the others.

"Krastin." Rhain let his voice echo through the ruins.

The scientists spun.

Krastin stepped forward. "Ah, Overlord, finally."

"It's you who will die here tonight," Rhain said.

They walked toward each other.

"We'll see," Krastin fired back.

MAL'S HEART was thumping like a bass drum as she crept toward Thadd.

She couldn't drag her eyes off Rhain and Krastin.

Krastin was much shorter than Rhain, and looked like he was no match for him.

Then the Zhylaw warlord stepped forward. Suddenly, six tentacle-like appendages burst from the man's back.

Mal gasped, horror gripping her. They looked like snakes, splaying out behind him. Each one had teeth on the end.

Of course, the Zhylaw would depend on their horrible enhancements, even on themselves.

Rhain drew his wicked swords and they lit up as he charged them with energy.

The men ran at each other.

Tentacles snapped at Rhain, biting and ripping his flesh. His swords slashed, and he sliced one tentacle off. But it instantly started to regrow.

No.

Rhain didn't look worried. He whirled and slashed. Krastin leaped out of the way, and they danced across the space.

Thadd. She had to get to Thadd.

Pulling her gaze off Rhain, she darted forward. She got closer and saw the terrible wounds on Thadd's chest.

Movement made her whip her sword up.

A female Zhylaw scientist froze, dark eyes wide. Mal glared at the woman, then the Zhylaw spun and raced away.

The woman wasn't Mal's priority. She hurried past the cages, and the hexids inside snarled and growled.

Their eyes were inky black and they threw themselves at the bars, mindless and hungry.

All these creatures wanted to do was tear and kill.

For a second, Mal wondered if these creatures remembered what they'd been, if who they once were was still inside them. Did they have any awareness of what they'd become?

She looked up at the hanging cage and Poppy's motionless form.

Mal's chest hitched. *Almost there, Poppy.*

She saw Herris and Zand under the cage. She trusted the fighters to get her friend down.

Mal circled the benches and saw other animals strapped down. She couldn't leave them. One was a dog-like creature with matted curly fur and large liquid eyes filled with pain. Mal sliced the bindings.

With a yip, the animal rolled off.

Oh boy, he was bigger than she'd guessed and reached above her waist.

It moved forward and she froze.

Then it licked her hand before it turned and bounded away into the darkness.

Right. She rubbed the slobber on her pants and kept moving. As she checked the other animals, she realized all of them were dead.

She finally reached Thadd and swallowed the bile in her throat.

"I'm here, Thadd," she whispered.

He turned his head. His gaze was hot and feverish, but she wasn't sure if he saw her or recognized her.

She untied the heavy bindings and unclipped the medical equipment attached to him. His chest was a raw, gaping wound. She swallowed hard. She couldn't move him like this.

Suddenly, a Zhylaw man rushed at her, with some medical device in his hand.

Mal leaped back and lifted her sword.

The scientist was trying to stop her from helping Thadd. Anger exploded. She slashed and cut across his arm, severing something vital. He dropped his makeshift weapon, his fingers nerveless. The man stared at the blood dripping off his fingers.

Mal stabbed her sword into his gut, then pulled it free. He collapsed with a gurgle.

She turned back to Thadd.

It was so wrong to see the strong captain so still and so in pain.

"Okay, Thadd." She held her palm over his chest. She needed to stop his bleeding.

She pulled on her energy and felt it swell around her. It was a trickle at first, but started to grow.

A part of her wondered how she'd gone her entire life without feeling it, when now, she couldn't imagine not feeling it.

It felt right. A part of her.

Her power grew and swelled. She had no idea how to heal, but in her head, she imagined Thadd's skin knitting closed.

He groaned.

Mal pressed her lips together and saw his chest starting to heal... Slowly, so slowly.

He groaned again. She knew that she was hurting him.

"I'm sorry." She felt a prick of tears.

Then she heard a giant crash.

She whipped her head around and saw Rhain and Krastin. Rhain was covered in bite marks from the tentacles. He slashed with his sword, moving so fast. Krastin was bleeding as well, from several cuts and two of his tentacles were severed.

The warlord charged at Rhain. They crashed into a cage, and the hexids inside went wild.

Mal bit her lip and turned back to Thadd. He wasn't fully healed yet and she poured more energy into him.

God, it hurt. Energy ripped out of her.

With another groan, Thadd's eyes opened. This time she saw vague awareness in them.

"Mal...?" His voice was a croaky whisper.

"We're here. We've got you, Thadd. We're getting out of here."

Her energy cut off. She couldn't do any more. His chest looked better, but nowhere near fully healed.

She helped the big man sit up.

He groaned. "I've...got it."

"Sure you do," she said.

She helped him off the table. He staggered and the weight of him almost sent them both crashing to the ground.

"Whoa. Just take a second." She spotted some

bandages, and grabbed them and started wrapping them around his bloodied chest. She'd need help to move him.

A fierce roar cut through the air. Rhain was airborne, swords held over his head.

Krastin dodged and his tentacles whipped out and wrapped around Rhain. Some stabbed at him, tearing flesh off.

Mal's gut clenched. *Come on, baby, take him down.*

Rhain let off a pulse of energy and Krastin flew backward.

Mal released a breath. She knew she couldn't move Thadd on her own. Herris and Zand had Poppy's cage lowered, and were busy trying to get it open.

Then she heard the roar of hungry animals and swiveled, her pulse racing.

She saw a female Zhylaw scientist unlocking the hexid cages.

Her heart jumped into her throat. *Asshole.* She'd kill them all.

The hexids burst free. Thadd leaned heavily on her. Herris and Zand were still busy with Poppy's cage. Rhain and Krastin were locked in battle.

Muscles flexing, the hexids loped toward the battling pair, raw hunger on their faces. No. *No.* She couldn't let them massacre her man and all the others.

She leaned Thadd back against the bench and then leaped up on top of a large box. She threw her hands out.

Energy burst from her. A wave of brilliant silver energy washed over the space, engulfing the hexids and Zhylaw.

All her fear, all her anger, and all the other warmer emotions she was starting to feel for Rhain flooded her.

The hexids and Zhylaw vanished, melting away into nothing.

Chest heaving, she stared in horror.

She turned, and saw Krastin staring at her in shock.

Rhain smiled, pride on his face.

CHAPTER SEVENTEEN

Rhain grinned at Mal. *His fierce woman.*

But then he saw Thadd behind her, hurt and injured.

Rhain turned to Krastin.

The Zhylaw looked like he'd seen a predator appear out of nowhere.

"You should have never come to my planet, Krastin. Never have touched my people."

The man rallied. "I will kill you, Sarkany, like I killed your mother. Your father will forgive me. I'll bury you deep and no one will ever find you."

"You also made a mistake touching my woman's friend. She will never forgive you, and she will make you pay."

Krastin backed up, his tentacles waving behind his back, several damaged by Rhain's swords.

Mal started advancing.

Krastin pulled out a blaster.

Rhain whipped his hand up. Energy shot from him

and yanked the weapon out of Krastin's hand. It flew through the air and hit a rock wall.

Mal jumped and sailed through the air. She was carried up by her energy, then she landed beside Rhain.

He'd never been prouder to know that she was his.

"You hurt my friends." Her eyes were glowing with silver light. "You attacked my man."

"You can't stop Zavir," Krastin bit out. "He'll keep coming."

"And we'll keep fighting him," Rhain said.

"You're his blood."

"He's nothing like your asshole boss," Mal snapped. "He's overlord Rhain Zhalto Sarkany. He's a good leader who protects his people." She raised her sword. It pulsed with silver energy. "You are a piece of shit who hurts other people, enslaves them. You hurt my friend. This is for Poppy."

She lunged. Krastin's tentacles snapped out, wrapping around her.

Rhain rushed in, slicing his sword through the protuberances.

Krastin screamed, his hands reaching for Mal. One tentacle slithered around her neck and pulled tight.

No. The *Gorr*-ridden Zhylaw *wouldn't* hurt her.

Rhain spun his blade and sank it into Krastin's midsection.

The warlord froze.

Mal ripped the tentacle free. She raised her sword, her face a mask of fury.

"Die, damn you." She sank her sword in beside Rhain's.

Krastin opened his mouth and coughed. Blood poured out.

Together, Rhain and Mal pulled their swords free.

The warlord staggered back, blood oozing from his wounds. His tentacles sagged.

Then Mal leaped up and sliced with her sword.

She cut through Krastin's neck, and his head rolled along the stony ground.

Then she looked up at Rhain. He'd never seen anything or anyone more beautiful. He yanked her to him and kissed her.

She kissed him back, filled with power and life.

They broke apart.

"Thadd needs help," she said.

He nodded and hurried with her over to where Thadd waited. His captain was in bad shape, leaning against a bench. Blood stained the bandages on his chest.

"Thadd." Rhain slid an arm around his best friend.

"I...missed the good part," Thadd rasped.

"Don't worry, Krastin is very dead. And Mal annihilated the hexids."

"Poppy," Mal cried.

Herris and Zand had the cage open. The small blonde woman lay on the ground, Herris kneeling beside her.

Gorr. Rhain hobbled over with Thadd. Mal dropped to her knees beside her friend and ran a hand over Poppy's dirty hair.

"Poppy, it's Mal. I'm here."

Poppy moaned, then her body shook, caught in a

seizure. Her back arched and she gave a horrible cry. Then her skin rippled.

Mal gasped and yanked her hand back.

Patches of gray fur flickered on Poppy's skin.

Auroras above. A second later, the fur disappeared and the woman slumped.

"What's wrong with her? What did they do to her?" Mal's eyes were panicked.

Rhain passed Thadd to Herris. He crouched and touched Mal's shoulder. "I don't know. We'll do what we can to help her."

"Look at her hands," Zand said.

Rhain saw that Poppy's fingers were tipped with sharp claws. A second later, the claws retracted.

"What the hell?" Mal whispered.

She leaped to her feet and spun. She spied a surviving Zhylaw scientist crouched behind some crates.

"You!" She strode over.

The man scrambled backward.

Mal grabbed the front of his shirt and yanked him up. He was a little shorter than she was.

"What did you do to her?"

"Nothing." The man shook his head. "I don't know."

Mal shook him.

"She wasn't one of my experiments!"

"She's not an experiment, you asshole. She's a living, breathing, sentient person."

The scientist whimpered.

"Who hurt her?" Mal demanded.

"Bexa. Um, you killed her."

"What did she do to my friend?"

"I don't know, but her other test subject is over there." He pointed to a cage at the end of the long row.

Mal dropped him and stalked forward. Rhain followed her.

The final cell held a huge form covered in gray fur. It was a nightmarish mix of man and beast, and he lay slumped on the floor. He had a long snout, huge, clawed hands, and dense fur.

"It's dead," Mal said. "What is it?"

Rhain stared, then met her gaze. "It's a Damari. A shapeshifter from the neighboring planet of Damar."

"Your brother's planet?"

"Yes. Poppy's been infected by a Damar."

Mal scraped a hand over her face.

Rhain pulled her close.

"Can we stop it?" she asked. "There must be *something* we can do." There was so much pain in her voice.

"There's nothing. The infection must run its course." He didn't tell her that many didn't survive the change.

Mal gripped him. "She'll be different?"

"A shapeshifter, yes."

He remembered the vision from the energy witch. She'd warned them that Poppy would be changed.

"God." Mal clung to him.

Poppy arched and screamed in agony.

Mal hurried back to her friend, dropping down and holding her hand. "I'm here, Poppy. You aren't alone."

Poppy's eyes opened. They were blue, and drowning in pain.

"Mal?" A faint whisper.

"Yes. I'm here. I'm here."

"We need to get her to Tavith." Rhain hoped the medica could ease her pain.

Thadd needed healing as well.

There was a sound, and he turned, lifting his swords. He saw his fighters appear, led by Carvia.

"Overlord, the Zhylaw are all defeated."

Thank the auroras. Rhain nodded. "Well done."

"We destroyed the comm jammer. Flyers are inbound from Citadel."

"Thank you, Carvia."

Rhain stood behind Mal, a hand on his woman's shoulder as they kept a vigil on her friend and waited for help.

MAL WATCHED the flyers descend in front of the ruins. The eastern horizon was just starting to light with dawn.

Around them lay dead Zhylaw and hexids, but she was too numb to feel anything. Rhain's fighters stood, watching the flyers land. Carvia waved them in.

Thadd and Poppy were resting on stretchers.

Thadd was awake, and clearly in pain, but he was alert and talking.

Poppy had suffered another seizure, and more fur had appeared on her body, but she was unconscious now.

Mal felt frozen inside. She felt so much guilt. She should've done more, something different, gotten to Poppy sooner.

"Mal?" Rhain appeared and pulled her close.

She leaned into him. "I don't want Poppy to die."

"Whatever she needs, we'll get help for her. I'll call Brodin. He'll help her."

The flyers touched down, and she saw Tavith and his team hurry off one.

The medica eyed Thadd. "Aracelle, help the captain and get him loaded on the flyer." Tavith moved to Poppy. He scanned her, his brow creased as he studied his wristband, a projection spearing up from it.

Poppy shifted restlessly and moaned.

"There, child. Easy." He pressed his palm to her forehead, then pulled out his kit. He applied a patch to Poppy's collarbone, and Mal watched it dissolve.

A second later, Poppy relaxed and went still.

"We need to get her back to Citadel," Tavith said. "How badly are you two hurt?"

"I'm fine," Mal said. "Poppy and Thadd need you more."

Tavith held his arm up and his band scanned her.

She blew out a breath.

"You have several minor injuries, and some recently healed internal ones."

Mal opened her mouth—

"In the flyer, Mallory. I'll have one of my team heal you." He grabbed her arm. "And I will do everything I can for your friend."

She sagged against Rhain. "Thank you, Tavith."

Tavith nodded, and followed Poppy's stretcher onto the flyer.

"Come on." Rhain helped Mal aboard.

On the flight back, a young female medica worked on

Mal, and then Rhain. Mal felt a lot better physically by the time Citadel and its gleaming walls and spires came into view.

But every time she looked at Poppy's still form, she felt hollow, carved out.

They finally landed, and she watched the medicas whisk Thadd and Poppy away. She took one step to follow, but Rhain grabbed her arm.

"There's nothing you can do to help them right now."

"But—"

"Let Tavith heal her. Let's go and get cleaned up."

Mal hesitated, then curled her fingers around his.

He led her to his suite. He strode past the big bed and straight into the bathroom. He slowly and methodically stripped her clothes off, and then his own.

It was finally sinking in that they'd survived.

Krastin was dead.

Mal released a shuddering breath. Thadd and Poppy were alive. That's what she had to hold onto.

Rhain pulled her into the huge shower.

The warm water felt like heaven, and a second later, a ray of light washed over them, and she watched the grime disappear off her skin.

She looked up into the rugged, masculine face, and the silver-gray eyes filled with promise.

"*Rhain.*"

He lowered his head and closed his mouth over hers.

She kissed him back, emotions filling every part of her. She hadn't realized how empty she'd been until this man had filled her up.

His grip tightened, and he lifted his head, raw need in his eyes.

"I love you," she whispered.

His eyes widened.

When he didn't say anything, fear gripped her. She'd never said the words to a man before. It was crazy to blurt them out now, way too soon.

She went to take a step back, but he slid a strong hand into her hair.

"You have no idea the things you make me feel." He nipped her lips, then his mouth ran down her neck. He bit her skin.

Mal cried out.

"You have no idea how much I love you, Mallory West."

Oh. Warmth filled her.

"Mine," he said.

"Yours. Always."

His mouth was on hers again. He backed her up until her back hit the cool wall of the shower.

"And you're mine," she said. "My Rhain."

"Yes."

How the hell had she gotten so lucky? Of course, she'd had to cross the universe to find the right man for her. But finally, the universe had stopped being a bitch and given her this gorgeous, loyal, amazing man.

She kissed his chest. She slid her hand down his wet abs and circled his heavy cock. She stroked and his groan echoed off the walls.

Then he shifted and lifted her, pinning her against the wall.

He nudged her with his cock, and his gaze met hers. With one thrust, he was inside her.

Mal clung to him and cried out his name.

"Mal. *Take me.*"

"Rhain, I need..."

"Tell me." He kept moving his hips, plunging deep inside her.

"*You*. I just need you."

"You have me," he told her.

His thrusts became harder, wilder. He slid a hand between their straining bodies and found her clit.

Mal bucked and splintered apart. She screamed, and felt her body clench on his cock.

Rhain turned into a wild man, driving deeper.

"I'm coming. *Gorr*, Mal—"

His big body arched, his cock lodged deep. He shuddered, his face twisting.

She watched the pleasure rock through him.

When he sagged against her, pinning her against the wall, she just held on. The feeling of connection felt too good. So right.

He nuzzled her neck. "I love you."

She sighed against him. "I love you too, Rhain."

He lifted his head, his face serious. "Stay. Stay with me."

Her belly clenched.

The fact was, she didn't want to be anywhere else.

With him, she belonged. With him, she knew someone cared if she was happy, sad, safe, or alive.

"I'll stay."

CHAPTER EIGHTEEN

Later that afternoon, Rhain walked Mal into the medica.

After their shower, they'd slept for several hours, wrapped up in his bed.

No, *their* bed. Mal had agreed to stay.

Now, he just had one more thing to convince her about.

The first thing he saw in the medica was Thadd. His captain was standing, dressed, and looked fit and healthy.

"Thadd." Rhain stepped forward.

His friend looked up. A small smile hit Thadd's lips. They hugged, and Rhain slapped Thadd's back.

"You're healed?"

"I'm absolutely fine." Thadd said the words fast.

Rhain studied his captain's face and he didn't miss the haunted look in the man's eyes. He stepped back so Mal could hug Thadd as well.

Rhain's gut contracted. Thadd might be physically

healed, but he wasn't over the horror of what the Zhylaw had done to him.

Tavith bustled over, grumbling.

"Captain Naveri would benefit from a few more days of rest."

A fierce scowl appeared on Thadd's face. "I can rest in my own bed."

Tavith crossed his arms. "We all know you won't stay in bed."

"I...need to keep busy."

Rhain kept his face blank. Mal grabbed his hand.

The medica studied Thadd for a moment, then sighed. "Fine."

Thadd nodded and strode out.

"Is he really okay?" Rhain asked.

"His body is healed and the Zhylaw tech has been removed." Tavith scraped a hand over his head. "His mind just needs a little time. It would help if he talked to someone."

Rhain sighed. "Talking isn't Thadd's favorite thing to do."

"I know, but it will help him heal."

Rhain nodded. "I'll keep an eye on him."

Mal shifted restlessly. "Poppy?"

Tavith's face settled into grave lines. "Come with me. She's through here."

The medica led them through a doorway. Rhain squeezed Mal's hand.

She sucked in a breath. The room was bright and airy, and the blonde woman was visible on the bed.

Poppy Ellison was a pretty woman. She'd been

bathed, and wore a pale medica gown. There were scanner patches pressed to her skin, and at the moment, she was resting peacefully.

"Hi, Poppy, it's Mal." At her friend's bedside, Mal took the woman's hand.

There was no response.

"How is she?" Rhain asked.

Tavith sighed. "She's undergoing the Damari transformation."

Rhain pressed his lips together. "We guessed as much. "

"We're keeping her sedated. She's in no pain."

"When will she be out of danger?" Mal asked.

Tavith spread his hands. "I don't know. The transformation should've passed by now. It seems it's responding to her Earth genetics differently. Her readings are confusing and unusual."

Mal gasped, and Rhain reached for her.

"I don't have the expertise to treat her," Tavith said. "For now, we'll keep her stable and pain-free."

"And then what?" Mal's voice rose.

"Then, we send her to people who can help her."

Mal frowned.

"The overlord has already contacted his brother on Damar."

She swiveled, her eyebrows rising. "When?"

"When you were sleeping," Rhain said. "Tavith believes the Damari can help Poppy."

Mal looked at her friend.

"My brother, Brodin is already en route. He'll take her back to Damar, to his healers."

Mal stroked Poppy's hair. "I don't want her to leave, but if it helps her get better..."

"It's the best choice," Rhain said.

Tavith nodded.

"All right," Mal murmured.

Rhain released a breath. She didn't mention leaving with Poppy. He'd half expected her to want to go.

"As soon as she's well, she comes home," Mal said.

Home. Warmth spread inside him. She'd called Zhalto her home. "Of course."

She moved to him and pressed her face to his chest.

"She will be fine." He prayed to the auroras that his words were true.

"I'll inform you when Emperor Sarkany arrives from Damar," Tavith said.

"Thanks, Tavith," Mal said.

Rhain led Mal out of the medica.

"Emperor?" she asked.

"Emperor Brodin Damar Sarkany, Emperor of the Damari shapeshifters."

He led her down the hall and up some stairs.

"Where are you taking me now?" she asked.

"You'll see."

He finally stopped in front of a door. "Mal?"

She faced him. "Yes?"

"You said you'd stay here with me."

She grabbed his hands. "Yes. I want to be with you. I happen to be crazy in love with you, your Overlordness."

He cupped her jaw. "Good."

She rolled her eyes.

"I have another question for you."

"Okay, fire away."

"Two actually." He took a deep breath and pulled something from his pocket. "On Zhalto, it's customary for a woman to wear an energy jewel the color of her husband's energy." He held up a silver chain with a thin jewel on it. It glowed vibrant red.

She blinked. "Energy jewel?"

"They're mined in the south."

She swallowed. "Husband?"

"Yes. Mallory West, would you be my wife?"

She pressed a hand to the base of her neck. "Wife?"

"Yes, husband and wife. It's common when people fall in love."

"I've barely gotten used to being in love. This is…a lot."

Rhain smiled. "We don't have to get married today." But he didn't want to wait too long either. He'd convince her. After she'd had time to settle into life on Zhalto.

"All right." She smiled. "God. Yes, I'll marry you, Rhain Zhalto Sarkany."

Elation filled him. He slipped the chain over her neck. She touched the jewel and smiled.

Rhain pulled her close and kissed her.

Then she froze. "Wait, if we get married—?"

"*When* we get married."

She swallowed.

And suddenly his fierce warrior looked a little scared.

"If you're the overlord, does that mean…?"

"That you'll be my queen? Yes. Queen Mallory West Zhalto."

Her mouth opened, closed. "Rhain, I'm a *combat* pilot. I'm not queen material."

"Mal, a queen is someone who serves the best interests of her planet and its people. She fights for them, protects them from their enemies. You've already done all of that."

"But I'm not Zhalton, and I'm not royal."

"It doesn't matter. Carvia and my fighters have already been spreading stories of your exploits far and wide." He took her hand and opened the door. He pulled her onto a balcony. "They love you already."

She stared wide-eyed. The Zhaltons of Citadel crowded the bridges, balconies, and terraces. They all cheered and waved their banners and flags of red and silver.

"Our colors." He lifted her hand and kissed it.

Below them, the crowd cheered louder.

"You're lucky I love you," she muttered. Then she steeled herself, turned, and waved.

MAL LOOKED at herself in the mirror a few hours later.

Queen Mallory.

Jeez.

She shook her head. Rusty would be laughing. Well, she wanted Rhain, so it came with the territory.

He was worth it.

She finished changing, and now wore leather pants and a bronze halter top that she'd tied on and knotted in place.

Rhain's brother would be arriving soon, so she wanted to look presentable. She left her hair in a ponytail and headed up to the landing platform.

She didn't want to send Poppy away, but she trusted Tavith's advice. If this was what was best for Poppy, to help her heal, it needed to be done.

She found Rhain already waiting. He'd left earlier to check in with his advisors and see Thadd.

Rhain smiled and pulled her close. "I missed you."

God, she'd missed him too. She'd gone soft. She'd gotten so used to having him there. It was still a little scary.

But she wouldn't give him up. Not ever, not even for the chance to go back to Earth.

She breathed deeply and smiled. Rhain's masculine scent hit her, mixed with the fragrant floral scent of Citadel.

"Brodin's ship is in orbit. His shuttle will be landing shortly."

She nodded. "And you're sure this is best for Poppy?"

"Yes. I assure you, Brodin is honorable. His people can help her."

"All right."

A moment later, the shuttle came into view. It wasn't elegant. This brown ship was built sturdy, with a squat body and long wings.

Thadd stepped out onto the landing platform, his sharp gaze on the ship.

It swept in to land in front of them, a wash of air kicking dust their way.

The door opened and the first man who stepped out was big. Huge.

He wasn't that much taller than Rhain, but he was built for power. He moved like a predator, easy and smooth, but ready to erupt. His gray shirt stretched over slabs of corded muscle, and leather sheathed powerful legs. He had a touch of gray fur on his belt. His hair was long and silver-white, tied at the back of his neck. He had an enormous axe resting on his back and his eyes were a vivid blue, a few shades lighter than Thadd's.

But as the man's powerful stare collided with hers, she could barely resist the urge to look away. A sheen rolled over his eyes, then it was gone. He looked at his brother.

"Rhain." His voice was a deep rumble. A smile broke out on his rugged face.

"Brodin."

The men embraced.

Behind Brodin, three people—two men and a woman—exited the shuttle.

They also moved with animal-like grace. The men were tall and strong, and the woman was tall as well, with long, black hair with a hint of a curl, and gold-brown skin.

She watched them with eyes that were so dark they almost looked black. They locked on Thadd and the pair glared at each other.

Hmm, story there.

"Brodin," Rhain said. "Meet my wife-to-be and future queen, Mallory West of Earth."

"Wife?" Brodin looked at her. "That was fast."

"I didn't force him," she said dryly. "Actually, it took him a bit to convince me."

Brodin's lips quirked. "Well, I can see the attraction."

She smiled back. "I think Rhain likes my skills with a sword best."

"I doubt that." Brodin took her hand, bent over and… sniffed her skin. "A Damari custom. Welcome, little sister."

Mal tipped her head. She liked him.

"This is my first Claw, Annora Rahl."

First Claw? It must be his equivalent to Thadd.

The dark-eyed woman nodded. "And my cleavers, Edvin and Jaston."

The men bowed their heads. There was no doubt they were all deadly.

A door opened behind them, and Tavith and another medica appeared, pushing a floating stretcher.

Mal's heart clenched. "Thank you for helping my friend, Brodin."

Brodin nodded, brows drawn as he looked at the stretcher.

"Poppy is so smart, a gifted scientist, a good friend."

The stretcher paused. Poppy rested under a sheet, eyes closed, so still and pale.

"She's very small." Brodin stepped closer and sniffed. "She's definitely infected by a Damari."

"Tavith has the body of the Damari we found in Krastin's cells," Rhain said. "I'm sorry he was killed."

Brodin's square jaw hardened. "No doubt one of our missing hunters. At least we can return his body to his family."

Tavith stepped forward. "We've stored the body in a cryo-container. With your permission, we'll have it loaded onto your shuttle."

"Thank you." Brodin looked at Poppy again, then Mal. "We'll help her through the transition. My healers will do whatever they can."

"Thank you," Mal said.

"Edvin, load up Dr. Ellison."

"Yes, Emperor."

Tavith followed Brodin's man.

Mal watched the stretcher and Poppy disappear into the ship.

"We can't stay," Brodin said. "I need to return to Damar." His jaw tightened. "It seems our father has sent a warlord to my planet as well, to 'convince' me to join him."

Rhain cursed.

"I will *never* stand at his side," Brodin growled. "And he will regret hurting my people."

Rhain clasped his brother's arm. "Whatever help you need, you have it from me."

"Thank you, brother. My fighters and I will hunt this dog down. Early intel suggests it is Candela Salix."

Rhain sucked in a breath. "Be careful, Brodin. That Zhylaw woman's expertise is in poisons."

"I'll watch my step, and she will regret ever stepping foot on Damar." Brodin looked at Rhain and Mal. "Rest easy now with your mate, Rhain. You've fought your battle."

"But the war isn't over until you and Gray, and all our planets, are safe."

"It won't be over until our father is dead."

"Be careful, Brodin. Good hunting."

A feral smile crossed the emperor's face. "I don't specialize in careful."

"Look after my friend," Mal said.

The man nodded. "We'll keep you informed of her progress. I hope to have her back to you, healthy and well, soon."

The big man stalked toward the shuttle, his people following him. He leaped aboard.

Moments later, the shuttle lifted off.

Rhain and Mal watched it ascend until it disappeared from the sky.

"God, I hope Poppy will be all right," Mal said.

"She will." He threaded his fingers with hers. "So, my lovely warrior, what shall we do now?"

She pressed against him. "Hmm, I can think of a thing or two." She let her energy out and it coiled around him.

He did the same, feeling their energies mix.

"Then lead the way, Mal. I will always be happy to walk at your side."

Her heart melted. Her man, her overlord, looked at her like she was both precious and fierce. She was right where she belonged and she was never letting him go.

CHAPTER NINETEEN

One week later

"Wider, Mal."

Rhain tugged her hair gently, loving the sound of her moan.

She was on her hands and knees in front of him. He was driving inside her with slow, steady thrusts.

Making a hungry sound, she pushed back against him.

"You love me inside you, don't you?" he said, voice rough, guttural.

"*Yes.*"

Over the last week, this bed had become theirs. And he'd watched her slowly relax into her new home.

Into them.

Every day, he made love to her. Every night, they slept together right here.

Rhain picked up speed. Her tight body clenched on his cock—wet, slick, and so good.

"*Mal.*" A deep groan. "Arch your back."

She did as he asked. He thrust harder, the sound of their flesh slapping together coming faster and faster. He felt his release building.

It wasn't enough.

It seemed he'd never get enough of this woman.

He pulled back.

Mal cried out in protest.

He spun her onto her back. He took a second to appreciate the view. Her dark hair spilled around her flushed face, her delicious breasts prominent, her taut stomach leading down to the dark curls between her thighs, that were damp with her need.

He shoved her sleek legs apart and sank back inside her.

She moaned, and wrapped her legs around his waist.

And there it was. All the emotion on her face—need, yearning.

Love.

"*Rhain*," she panted.

He picked up speed. He slid a hand down and found that little, swollen nub he loved to lavish with attention.

He felt his energy spill loose and hers rose to meet it.

It kept them in a snug cocoon of power as the pleasure grew inside them both.

"Now, Mal. *Now*."

Her body arched up, her hips lifting into his hard thrusts.

Rhain watched his woman come, taking his cock, and heard the sweet noises that he wanted to hear for the rest of his life.

Then his own orgasm hit hard.

His next thrust was deep, brutal. He grunted, pleasure detonating inside him.

Rhain still had enough thought to drop down beside her on the bed, rather than on top of her.

She didn't move, so he pulled her close, tucking her sweat-slicked body against his. He ran his hand down her back and cupped her ass cheek.

"Still nervous?" he asked.

"Hmm?"

He wasn't sure she'd even heard him.

"About the banquet? Are you still nervous?"

Mal sat bolt upright. "The banquet." She groaned and dropped flat on her back on the bed, and threw an arm over her eyes.

He tugged her arm away. "Where is my tough, hexid-killing warrior from Earth? Surely, she can wear a dress, dance, and smile at people?"

"Dance? I don't dance, Rhain."

"You'll be fine." He pushed off the bed.

"You never said anything about dancing," she said unhappily.

"I'll help you." He leaned over her and pressed a quick kiss to her sulky mouth. "I'll be right by your side the entire time. Your people want to meet their future queen."

She didn't go quite as pale and wide-eyed at the word queen now.

"Did you hear from Brodin?" she asked.

Rhain sighed. "Yes. He's coming to the banquet, and

yes, you can ask him yourself, but there's been no change. Poppy's alive, and that's what's important."

Mal nodded.

For a week, Poppy had been on Damar, but she remained unconscious.

"She doesn't appear to be going through a full Damari transformation. Her body is changing, but not in the usual ways." He cupped Mal's jaw. "Brodin's best healers are monitoring her."

"I know."

"Okay, time to shower. I've arranged a dress for you."

She groaned and pushed off the bed, uncaring that she was naked.

He loved that long, fit body. Loved even more that the bruises from the battle with Krastin had faded.

"I don't like dresses," she whined.

"Enough complaining, woman." He urged her into the bathroom.

After they showered, Rhain dressed in traditional Zhalton battle dress. His chest was bare, only covered by a leather harness. His battle skirt hit at his knees, meeting the supple leather of his boots. A wide belt circled his waist, threaded with the royal red color of his energy.

He left Mal with a handmaiden to finish getting ready. He checked with his advisors on the banquet preparation, and the arrival of the special guests.

He found Thadd organizing security. His captain was dressed much the same as Rhain, and looked his regular self, but Rhain still felt something wasn't quite right with his friend.

"Everything going smoothly?" Rhain asked.

Thadd nodded. "The guards are in position."

"After Krastin's defeat, I don't think my father will cause more trouble here on Zhalto." Rhain frowned. "Besides, he appears to have switched his focus to Damar."

Brodin had more missing hunters, and reports of the warlord Candela Salix lurking on his planet.

"Zavir won't set foot in Citadel," Thadd promised darkly.

Rhain gripped his captain's arm. "Thadd, if you need to talk..."

"I'm fine." Thadd looked away. "I need to check on some more things. I'll see you at the banquet."

Rhain watched him go. He vowed that he would get Thadd to open up, one way or another.

Then he heard the click of heels.

He turned and his heart stopped.

Mal walked toward him.

He'd selected the red dress, knowing that it would look wonderful on her.

But he hadn't been prepared for this.

The fabric looked like liquid on her. The deep V neck showcased her gorgeous breasts and the energy jewel she wore, and the bodice was overlaid with silver metalwork that nipped in at her waist. The full skirt draped to the floor, but two long slits up each side showed off her long legs with each step. Her dark hair was piled up on top of her head, with a silver flower tucked behind her ear.

Rhain just stared.

Mal stopped in front of him, her gaze running over his chest. "I really like your outfit."

He kept staring at her.

"You look like you just got hit in the head," she said.

"You look...incredible."

Her lips quirked. "It's a hell of a dress. Thank you for picking something I'd like."

"You're a beautiful woman. I prefer you naked—"

She snorted.

"—but you look beautiful in this." He yanked her to him. "I'm proud to have such a beautiful, strong, smart, and brave woman agree to be mine."

A woman whose presence in his life meant he didn't need to fear the darkness. There was no way he'd leave her to embrace his father's way of life. And there was no way she'd let him. He knew she'd always fight for him, help him, and stand at his side.

She melted against him. "Just keep looking at me just like that."

"I will, every day for the rest of our lives."

MAL SIPPED her drink and looked across the elegant ballroom.

The tall, arched windows framed the auroras lighting up the night sky. Inside, there were flowers everywhere—mostly silver and red.

Carvia stood beside her in a column of blue. "Are you enjoying all this fuss?"

Mal smiled at the fighter and held her glass out. The other woman clinked hers against it.

"More than I thought I would."

All of Citadel society was here. The women wore beautiful dresses, while the men were bare chested, with leather harnesses. People were dancing at the far end of the hall to some beautiful, evocative music. The dancers dipped and twirled in elegant moves that Mal was certain she couldn't do.

"My lady?" A server appeared, tray in hand.

Mal realized the man was talking to her. "Yes."

"From the overlord." The man lifted the tray.

On a small silver tray rested...some roasted nuts. She grinned and nabbed a handful. She popped them into her mouth, salty flavor exploding. Not quite the same as peanuts, but close.

She spied Rhain not far away in the crowd.

God, he was handsome. His muscles gleamed under the lights, as did the medallion on his chest.

Like he sensed her, his head lifted. When he saw what she was eating, he smiled.

She smiled back. Love swamped her. Man, she wanted to drag him out of there.

"You look at the overlord with such emotion," Carvia said.

Mal cleared her throat, hoping not *all* her thoughts showed. "I love him." She shook her head. "Apparently I had to crash land on the other side of the galaxy to find the right guy."

A sad smile crossed Carvia's face. "I'm very happy for you and him."

The woman's tone was loaded with unsaid feelings.

"You were in love with Trist," Mal said quietly.

The fighter looked at her shoes. "I never found the courage to tell him. I thought we'd have time."

Mal touched the woman's hand. "I'm sorry. I like to think that he knows now."

The woman nodded. "If the auroras grant me another chance, I won't waste my time." She glanced up. "Oh, the overlord's brothers have arrived."

Mal turned. She instantly recognized Brodin—big and powerful, that wild energy pumping off him.

The man beside him had to be Graylan.

He was tall, but leaner. He was still all muscle, not an ounce of fat on him. If Brodin was a giant wolf, Graylan was a sleek, black panther. He had a long, sharp face, and his black hair was cut short.

Rhain moved toward the men, smiling. Mal nodded goodbye to Carvia and walked through the crowd.

Graylan spotted her first. He had molten-gold eyes, and they flared as he took her in.

Rhain turned. "Ah, here's Mal now."

He held out his hand, and she took it.

"Mal," Brodin rumbled. Behind him, she saw his first claw, Annora. The woman wore a short aquamarine dress that showed off killer legs. She was trading yet another glare with Thadd.

"It's nice to see you again, Brodin," Mal said. "How's Poppy?"

"I suspected that would be the first thing you asked me." He took her hand and squeezed. "She opened her eyes today."

Mal gasped.

"She didn't speak. But my healers believe she's rising to consciousness."

"Thank God."

Rhain hugged her.

"Thank you for taking care of her," Mal whispered.

Brodin inclined his head.

"Mal," Rhain said. "This is my other brother, Conqueror Graylan Taln Sarkany."

The lean, dark Graylan held out his hand. "My brother chose well."

She took the man's hand and felt the throb of contained power. He looked dark and dangerous.

"We didn't really choose, it just happened," she said.

Rhain stroked a hand down her hair.

"In fact, he tied me up and interrogated me when we first met."

Rhain groaned, and his brothers laughed.

"I believe I atoned for my error."

She smiled up at him. "You did."

"We're happy that you found a beautiful, accomplished mate," Brodin said.

"Thank you." Rhain eyed them both. "How are things on your worlds?'

Brodin scowled. "I have more missing people. We continue to search for Candela."

Graylan's eyes flashed. "If Zavir or his proxies come anywhere near Taln, I will obliterate them."

Mal clutched Rhain's hand. Graylan was several levels above intense, and more than a little scary.

"Tonight, I hope you can relax. Go, eat, drink, dance with the ladies." Rhain pulled Mal closer. "I'm going to dance with my woman."

Mal groaned, but followed him to the dance floor.

The music slowed, and she followed his lead. Thankfully the steps were simple, and when she stepped on his foot, she laughed.

"I warned you."

"I can handle it." He tugged her closer.

"Thanks for the roasted nuts."

"My pleasure." He pressed his cheek to her hair. "This, having you right here, makes everything worthwhile."

Mal felt a surprising prick of tears. *Ack*. She wasn't going to cry. "I love you, Rhain. And I really think I'll come to love your planet, too."

She was already falling for it. She trained daily with Thadd, learning to wield her charged sword. Rhain was having her own set of kilwar blades crafted just for her. She sat in some of the classrooms with the school children, learning the history of Zhalto. She wandered the markets, buying loads of flowers and instruments she didn't need. And she'd already taken a flyer up for a flight, and she planned to go flying whenever she could.

"It's your home now," Rhain murmured.

Warmth filled her. God, if Rusty could see her now, he'd bust his gut laughing. In love, all dressed up, and dancing with an alien king to the scent of flowers in the air and colorful auroras in the sky.

Rusty had always said that happiness was a new pair

of cowboy boots. She grinned. He'd gotten that one wrong. Happiness was finding your place. It was loving and being loved.

"Mal?" Rhain said.

"Yes?" There was a weird note to his voice.

"Some other special guests have arrived."

She frowned and followed his gaze.

Two couples had entered the ballroom. The first man was powerfully built, with a touch of gray at his temples and a black eye patch on his rugged face. He wore a leather harness over his fitted black shirt, and a black cloak that fell from broad shoulders.

The man beside him was a little younger, and all corded muscle with a red cloak. His bare, bronze skin was covered in intricate tattoos.

Then she noticed the women with the men.

Mal froze. She'd seen pictures of these women before.

They were both tall and athletic. One had honey-brown hair in a braid and bronze skin. She wore an elegant, blue dress that fitted over her baby bump. The other woman had dark hair that she'd left loose, and a black dress that showed off her toned body.

They were both from Earth.

The pregnant woman was Sam Santos, former head of security for the Fortuna Space Station. She was now married to Galen, head of the House of Galen, on the desert world of Carthago.

The other woman was one of her security officers, Harper Adams. Her man was the champion gladiator of the Kor Magna Arena, Raiden Tiago.

A riot of feelings filled Mal. She didn't know these women, but they were from Earth. They'd been through a similar experience to her.

They'd survived, and more than that, they'd thrived.

Rhain stroked a hand down her back. "Go."

"Thank you," she said. "For bringing them here."

He brushed his thumb over her lips. "I'll do anything to make you happy, Mal."

She kissed him and then hurried over to the newcomers.

The men smiled politely, but Sam and Harper met her partway with huge grins.

"Mallory?" Sam said.

"It's Mal. Mal West."

"It's nice to meet you, Mal." Sam hugged her. "I'm Sam."

"And I'm Harper." The brunette hugged her, as well.

"I know we don't really know each other." Mal shook her head. "But it is *really* good to see you both."

"We get it." Sam squeezed Mal's hand. "One hundred percent."

"You're well?" Harper asked. "We were hoping you'd come to live on Carthago with us, but the overlord gave us an emphatic no."

"I'm good." Mal looked at Rhain. "This is going to be my home."

Sam smiled. "I see. It looks like you've done very well."

Mal looked past the women to the gladiators. "You too."

"So," Harper said. "If he's the overlord of this planet, does that mean you're going to be queen?"

Mal winced. "Um, yes, but I'm still not used to that bit yet."

The women laughed.

Rhain arrived, and slid his arm around her. "Welcome to Zhalto."

Imperator Galen stepped forward. "Thank you for the invitation."

"Come," Rhain said. "The food is being served."

It was much later, as the banquet was winding down, that Mal stood on a small balcony, watching the auroras dance. Rhain stood behind her, his arms wrapped around her.

The night had been perfect. They'd eaten, danced, and she'd spent hours talking with Sam and Harper. She felt a strong sense of connection to the women, and it filled something inside her.

She was far from Earth, but she wasn't far from home. Home was a feeling, not a place.

"Hey." Rhain nuzzled her neck.

"Thank you for tonight."

"It's been my pleasure."

He spun her and kissed her, and everything faded away.

She kissed him back and tasted him, *her Rhain*, and felt the powerful pulse of their energies.

"You can't get away now," he murmured. "I'm *very* glad you crashed on my planet, Mallory West of Earth."

"Me too."

"I love you."

"And I love you too, my Overlordness. Now, always, and wherever we are in the galaxy."

I hope you enjoyed Mal and Rhain's story!

I absolutely loved writing their adventure and **GALACTIC KINGS** continues with **EMPEROR** (Brodin's story) coming next month on the 18th of January 2022.

If you'd like to know more about Harper and Raiden, and Sam and Imperator Galen, then check out my action-packed science-fiction romance series, *Galactic Gladiators*. **Read on for a preview of *Gladiator*, the first book in Galactic Gladiators, starring Harper and Raiden.**

Don't miss out! For updates about new releases, action romance info, free books, and other fun stuff, sign up for my VIP mailing list and get your *free box set* containing three action-packed romances.

Visit here to get started: www.annahackett.com

PREVIEW: GLADIATOR

Just another day at the office.

Harper Adams pulled herself along the outside of the space station module. She could hear her quiet breathing inside her spacesuit, and she easily pulled her weightless body along the slick, white surface of the module. She stopped to check a security panel, ensuring all the systems were running smoothly.

Check. Same as it had been yesterday, and the day before that. But Harper never ever let herself forget that they were six hundred million kilometers away from Earth. That meant they were dependent only on themselves. She tapped some buttons on the security panel before closing the reinforced plastic cover. She liked to dot all her *I*s and cross all her *T*s. She never left anything to chance.

She grabbed the handholds and started pulling herself up over the cylindrical pod to check the panels on the other side. Glancing back behind herself, she caught a beautiful view of the planet below.

Harper stopped and made herself take it all in. The orange, white, and cream bands of Jupiter could take your breath away. Today, she could even see the famous superstorm of the Great Red Spot. She'd been on the Fortuna Research Station for almost eighteen months. That meant, despite the amazing view, she really didn't see it anymore.

She turned her head and looked down the length of the space station. At the end was the giant circular donut that housed the main living quarters and offices. The main ring rotated to provide artificial gravity for the residents. Lying off the center of the ring was the long cylinder of the research facility, and off that cylinder were several modules that housed various scientific labs and storage. At the far end of the station was the docking area for the supply ships that came from Earth every few months.

"Lieutenant Adams? Have you finished those checks?"

Harper heard the calm voice of her fellow space

marine and boss, Captain Samantha Santos, through the comm system in her helmet.

"Almost done," Harper answered.

"Take a good look at the botany module. The computer's showing some strange energy spikes, but the scientists in there said everything looks fine. Must be a system malfunction."

Which meant the geek squad engineers were going to have to come in and do some maintenance. "On it."

Harper swung her body around, and went feet-first down the other side of the module. She knew the rest of the security team—all made up of United Nations Space Marines—would be running similar checks on the other modules across the station. They had a great team to ensure the safety of the hundreds of scientists aboard the station. There was also a dedicated team of engineers that kept the guts of the station running.

She passed a large, solid window into the module, and could see various scientists floating around benches filled with all kinds of plants. They all wore matching gray jumpsuits accented with bright-blue at the collars, that indicated science team. There was a vast mix of scientists and disciplines aboard—biologists, botanists, chemists, astronomers, physicists, medical experts, and the list went on. All of them were conducting experiments, and some were searching for alien life beyond the edge of the solar system. It seemed like every other week, more probes were being sent out to hunt for radio signals or collect samples.

Since humans had perfected large solar sails as a way to safely and quickly propel spacecraft, getting around the solar system had become a lot easier. With radiation pressure exerted by sunlight onto the mirrored sails, they could travel from Earth to Fortuna Station orbiting Jupiter in just a few months. And many of the scientists aboard the station were looking beyond the solar system, planning manned expeditions farther and farther away. Harper wasn't sure they were quite ready for that.

She quickly checked the adjacent control panel. Among all the green lights, she spotted one that was blinking red, and she frowned. They definitely had a problem with the locking system on the exterior door at the end of the module. She activated the small propulsion pack on her spacesuit, and circled around the module. She slowed down as she passed the large, round exterior door at the end of the cylindrical module.

It was all locked into place and looked secure.

As she moved back to the module, she grabbed a handhold and then tapped the small tablet attached to the forearm of her suit. She keyed in a request for maintenance to come and check it.

She looked up and realized she was right near another window. Through the reinforced glass, a pretty, curvy blonde woman looked up and spotted Harper. She smiled and waved. Harper couldn't help but smile and lifted her gloved hand in greeting.

Dr. Regan Forrest was a botanist and a few years younger than Harper. The young woman was so open and friendly, and had befriended Harper from her first day on the station. Harper had never had a lot of friends —mainly because she'd been too busy raising her younger sister and working. She'd never had time for girly nights out or gossip.

But Regan was friendly, smart, and had the heart of a steamroller under her pretty exterior. Harper always had trouble saying no to her. Maybe the woman reminded her a little of Brianna. At the thought of her sister, something twisted painfully in Harper's chest.

Regan floated over to the window and held up a small tablet. She'd typed in some words.

Cards tonight?

Harper had been teaching Regan how to play poker. The woman was terrible at it, and Harper beat her all the time. But Regan never gave up.

Harper nodded and held up two fingers to indicate a couple of hours. She was off-shift shortly, and then she had a sparring match with Regan's cousin, Rory—one of the station engineers—in the gym. Aurora "Call me Rory or I'll hit you" Fraser had been trained in mixed martial arts, and Harper found the female engineer a hell of a sparring partner. Rory was teaching Harper some martial arts moves and Harper was showing the woman some basic sword moves. Since she was little, Harper had been a keen fencer.

Regan grinned back and nodded. Then the woman's wide smile disappeared. She spun around, and through the glass Harper could see the other scientists all looking around, concerned. One scientist was spinning around, green plants floating in the air around him, along with fat droplets of water and some other green fluid. He'd clearly screwed up and let his experiment get free.

"Lieutenant Adams?" The captain's voice came through her helmet again. "Harper?"

There was a sense of urgency that made Harper's belly tighten. "Go ahead, Captain."

"We have an alarm sounding in the botany module. The computer says there is a risk of decompression."

Dammit. "I just checked the security panels. The locking mechanism on the exterior door is showing red. I did a visual inspection and it's closed up tight."

"Okay, we talked with the scientist in charge. Looks like one of her team let something loose in there. It isn't dangerous, but it must be messing with the alarm sensors. System's locked them all in there." She made an annoyed sound. "Idiots will have to stay there until engineering can get down there and free them."

Harper studied the room through the glass again. Some of the green liquid had floated over to another bench that contained various frothing cylinders on it. A second later, the cylinders shattered, their contents bubbling upward.

The scientists all moved to the back exit of the module, banging on the locked door. *Damn.* They were trapped.

Harper met Regan's gaze. Her friend's face was pale, and wisps of her blonde hair had escaped her ponytail, floating around her face.

"Captain," Harper said. "Something's wrong. The experiments have overflowed their containment." She could see the scientists were all coughing.

"Engineering is on the way," the captain said.

Harper pushed herself off, flying over the surface of

the module. She reached the control panel and saw that several other lights had turned red. They needed to get this under control and they needed to do it now.

"Harper!" The captain's panicked voice. "Decompression in progress!"

What the hell? The module jerked beneath Harper. She looked up and saw the exterior door blow off, flying away from the station.

Her heart stopped. That meant all the scientists were exposed to the vacuum of space.

Fuck. Harper pushed off again, sending herself flying toward the end of the module. She put her arms by her sides to help increase her speed. Through the window, she saw that most of the scientists had grabbed on to whatever they could hold on to. A few were pulling emergency breathers over their heads.

She reached the end of the pod and saw the damage. There was torn metal where the door had been ripped off. Inside the door, she knew there would be a temporary repair kit containing a sheet of high-tech nano fabric that could be stretched across the opening to reestablish pressure. But it needed to be put in place manually. Harper reached for the latch to release the repair kit.

Suddenly, a slim body shot out of the pod, her arms and legs kicking. Her mouth was wide open in a silent scream.

Regan. Harper didn't let herself think. She turned, pushed off and fired her propulsion system, arrowing after her friend.

"Security Team to the botany module," she yelled through her comm system. "Security Team to botany module. We have decompression. One scientist has been expelled. I'm going after her. I need someone that can help calm the others and get the module sealed again."

"Acknowledged, Lieutenant," Captain Santos answered. "I'm on my way."

Harper focused on reaching Regan. She was gaining on her. She saw that the woman had lost consciousness. She also knew that Regan had only a couple of minutes to survive out here. Harper let her training take over. She tapped the propulsion system controls, trying for more speed, as she maneuvered her way toward Regan.

As she got close, Harper reached out and wrapped her arm around the scientist. "I've got you."

Harper turned, at the same time clipping a safety line to the loops on Regan's jumpsuit. Then, she touched the controls and propelled them straight back towards the module. She kept her friend pulled tightly toward her chest. *Hold on, Regan.*

She was so still. It reminded Harper of holding Brianna's dead body in her arms. Harper's jaw tightened. She wouldn't let Regan die out here. The woman had dreamed of working in space, and worked her entire career to get here, even defying her family. Harper wasn't going to fail her.

As the module got closer, she saw that the security team had arrived. She saw the captain's long, muscled body as she and another man put up the nano fabric.

"Incoming. Keep the door open."

"Can't keep it open much longer, Adams," the captain replied. "Make it snappy."

Harper adjusted her course, and, a second later, she

shot through the door with Regan in her arms. Behind her, the captain and another huge security marine, Lieutenant Blaine Strong, pulled the stretchy fabric across the opening.

"Decompression contained," the computer intoned.

Harper released a breath. On the panel beside the door, she saw the lights turning green. The nano fabric wouldn't hold forever, but it would do until they got everyone out of here, and then got a maintenance team in here to fix the door.

"Oxygen levels at required levels," the computer said again.

"Good work, Lieutenant." Captain Sam Santos floated over. She was a tall woman with a strong face and brown hair she kept pulled back in a tight ponytail. She had curves she kept ruthlessly toned, and golden skin she always said was thanks to her Puerto Rican heritage.

"Thanks, Captain." Harper ripped her helmet off and looked down at Regan.

Her blonde hair was a wild tangle, her face was pale and marked by what everyone who worked in space called space hickeys—bruises caused by the skin's small blood vessels bursting when exposed to the vacuum of space. *Please be okay.*

"Here." Blaine appeared, holding a portable breather. The big man was an excellent marine. He was about six foot five with broad shoulders that stretched his spacesuit to the limit. She knew he was a few inches over the height limit for space operations, but he was a damn good marine, which must have gone in his favor. He had dark skin thanks to his African-American father and his handsome face made him popular with the station's single ladies, but mostly he worked and hung out with the other marines.

"Thanks." Harper slipped the clear mask over Regan's mouth.

"Nice work out there." Blaine patted her shoulder. "She's alive because of you."

Suddenly, Regan jerked, pulling in a hard breath.

"You're okay." Harper gripped Regan's shoulder. "Take it easy."

Regan looked around the module, dazed and panicky. Harper watched as Regan caught sight of the fabric stretched across the end of the module, and all the plants floating around inside.

"God," Regan said with a raspy gasp, her breath fogging up the dome of the breather. She shook her head, her gaze moving to Harper. "Thanks, Harper."

"Any time." Harper squeezed her friend's shoulder. "It's what I'm here for."

Regan managed a wan smile. "No, it's just you. You didn't have to fly out into space to rescue me. I'm grateful."

"Come on. We need to get you to the infirmary so they can check you out. Maybe put some cream on your hickeys."

"Hickeys?" Regan touched her face and groaned. "Oh, no. I'm going to get a ribbing."

"And you didn't even get them the pleasurable way."

A faint blush touched Regan's cheeks. "That's right. If I had, at least the ribbing would have been worth it."

With a relieved laugh, Harper looked over at her captain. "I'm going to get Regan to the infirmary."

The other woman nodded. "Good. We'll meet you back at the Security Center."

With a nod, Harper pushed off, keeping one arm around Regan, and they floated into the main part of the science facility. Soon, they moved through the entrance into the central hub of the space station. As the artificial gravity hit, Harper's boots thudded onto the floor. Beside her, Regan almost collapsed.

Harper took most of the woman's weight and helped her down the corridor. They pushed into the infirmary.

A gray-haired, barrel-chested man rushed over. "Decided to take an unscheduled spacewalk, Dr. Forrest?"

Regan smiled weakly. "Yes. Without a spacesuit."

The doctor made a tsking sound and then took her from Harper. "We'll get her all patched up."

Harper nodded. "I'll come and check on you later."

Regan grabbed her hand. "We have a blackjack game scheduled. I'm planning to win back all those chocolates you won off me."

Harper snorted. "You can try." It was good to see some life back in Regan's blue eyes.

As Harper strode out into the corridor, she ran a hand through her dark hair, tension slowly melting out of her shoulders. She really needed a beer. She tilted her neck one way and then the other, hearing the bones pop.

Just another day at the office. The image of Regan drifting away from the space station burst in her head.

Harper released a breath. She was okay. Regan was safe and alive. That was all that mattered.

With a shake of her head, Harper headed toward the Security Center. She needed to debrief with the captain and clock off. Then she could get out of her spacesuit and take the one-minute shower that they were all allotted.

That was the one thing she missed about Earth. Long, hot showers.

And swimming. She'd been a swimmer all her life and there were days she missed slicing through the water.

She walked along a long corridor, meeting a few people—mainly scientists. She reached a spot where there was a long bank of windows that afforded a lovely view of Jupiter, and space beyond it.

Stingy showers and unscheduled spacewalks aside, Harper had zero regrets about coming out into space. There'd been nothing left for her on Earth, and to her surprise, she'd made friends here on Fortuna.

As she stared out into the black, mesmerized by the twinkle of stars, she caught a small flash of light in the distance. She paused, frowning. What the hell was that?

She stared hard at the spot where she'd seen the flash. Nothing there but the pretty sprinkle of stars. Harper shook her head. Fatigue was playing tricks on her. It had to have just been a weird trick of the lights reflecting off the glass.

Pushing the strange sighting away, she continued on to the Security Center.

Galactic Gladiators

Gladiator

OVERLORD

Warrior
Hero
Protector
Champion
Barbarian
Beast
Rogue
Guardian
Cyborg
Imperator
Hunter
Also Available as Audiobooks!

PREVIEW: EON WARRIORS AND HELL SQUAD

Looking for more action-packed science fiction romance? Check out *Eon Warriors,* starting with the first book in the series is *Edge of Eon.*

Framed for a crime she didn't commit, a wrongly-imprisoned space captain's only chance at freedom is to abduct a fearsome alien war commander.

Sub-Captain Eve Traynor knows a suicide mission when she sees one. With deadly insectoid aliens threatening to invade Earth, the planet's only chance of survival is to get the attention of the fierce Eon Warriors. But the Eon want nothing to do with Earth, and Eve wants nothing to do with abducting War Commander Davion Thann-Eon off his warship. But when Earth's Space Corps threaten her sisters, Eve will do anything to keep them safe, even if it means she might not make it back.

War Commander Davion Thann-Eon is taking his first vacation in years. Dedicated to keeping the Eon Empire safe, he's been born and bred to protect. But when he's attacked and snatched off his very own warship, he is shocked to find himself face-to-face with a bold, tough little Terran warrior. One who both infuriates and intrigues him.

When their shuttle is attacked by the ravenous insectoid Kantos, Eve and Davion crash land on the terrifying hunter planet known as Hunter7. A planet designed to test a warrior to his limits. Now, the pair must work together to survive, caught between the planet and its dangers, the Kantos hunting them down, and their own incendiary attraction.

Eon Warriors

Edge of Eon

Touch of Eon

Heart of Eon

Kiss of Eon

Mark of Eon

Claim of Eon

Storm of Eon

Soul of Eon
King of Eon
Also Available as Audiobooks!

Want to learn more about *Hell Squad*? Check out the first action-packed book in the series, *Marcus*.

In the aftermath of a deadly alien invasion, a band of survivors fights on…

In a world gone to hell, Elle Milton—once the darling of the Sydney social scene—has carved a role for herself as the communications officer for the toughest commando team fighting for humanity's survival—Hell Squad. It's her chance to make a difference and make up for horrible past mistakes...despite the fact that its battle-hardened commander never wanted her on his team.

When Hell Squad is tasked with destroying a strategic alien facility, Elle knows they need her skills in the field. But first she must go head to head with Marcus Steele and convince him she won't be a liability.

Marcus Steele is a warrior through and through. He fights to protect the innocent and give the human race a chance to survive. And that includes the beautiful, gutsy Elle who twists him up inside with a single look. The last thing he wants is to take her into a warzone, but soon they are thrown together battling both the alien invaders and their overwhelming attraction. And Marcus will learn just how much he'll sacrifice to keep her safe.

Hell Squad

Marcus

Cruz

Gabe

Reed

Roth

Noah

Shaw

Holmes

Niko

Finn

Devlin

Theron

Hemi

Ash

Levi

Manu

Griff

Dom

Survivors

Tane

Also Available as Audiobooks!

ALSO BY ANNA HACKETT

Norcross Security

The Investigator

The Troubleshooter

The Specialist

The Bodyguard

The Hacker

The Powerbroker

Billionaire Heists

Stealing from Mr. Rich

Blackmailing Mr. Bossman

Hacking Mr. CEO

Team 52

Mission: Her Protection

Mission: Her Rescue

Mission: Her Security

Mission: Her Defense

Mission: Her Safety

Mission: Her Freedom

Mission: Her Shield

Mission: Her Justice

Also Available as Audiobooks!

Treasure Hunter Security

Undiscovered

Uncharted

Unexplored

Unfathomed

Untraveled

Unmapped

Unidentified

Undetected

Also Available as Audiobooks!

Eon Warriors

Edge of Eon

Touch of Eon

Heart of Eon

Kiss of Eon

Mark of Eon

Claim of Eon

Storm of Eon

Soul of Eon

King of Eon

Also Available as Audiobooks!

Galactic Gladiators: House of Rone

Sentinel

Defender

Centurion

Paladin

Guard

Weapons Master

Also Available as Audiobooks!

Galactic Gladiators

Gladiator

Warrior

Hero

Protector

Champion

Barbarian

Beast

Rogue

Guardian

Cyborg

Imperator

Hunter

Also Available as Audiobooks!

Hell Squad

Marcus

Cruz

Gabe

Reed

Roth

Noah

Shaw

Holmes

Niko

Finn

Devlin

Theron

Hemi

Ash

Levi

Manu

Griff

Dom

Survivors

Tane

Also Available as Audiobooks!

The Anomaly Series

Time Thief

Mind Raider

Soul Stealer

Salvation

Anomaly Series Box Set

The Phoenix Adventures

Among Galactic Ruins

At Star's End

In the Devil's Nebula

On a Rogue Planet

Beneath a Trojan Moon

Beyond Galaxy's Edge

On a Cyborg Planet

Return to Dark Earth

On a Barbarian World

Lost in Barbarian Space

Through Uncharted Space

Crashed on an Ice World

Perma Series

Winter Fusion

A Galactic Holiday

Warriors of the Wind

Tempest

Storm & Seduction

Fury & Darkness

Standalone Titles

Savage Dragon

Hunter's Surrender

One Night with the Wolf

For more information visit www.annahackett.com

ABOUT THE AUTHOR

I'm a USA Today bestselling romance author who's passionate about ***fast-paced, emotion-filled*** contemporary romantic suspense and science fiction romance. I love writing about people overcoming unbeatable odds and achieving seemingly impossible goals. I like to believe it's possible for all of us to do the same.

I live in Australia with my own personal hero and two very busy, always-on-the-move sons.

For release dates, behind-the-scenes info, free books, and other fun stuff, sign up for the latest news here:

Website: www.annahackett.com

Printed in Great Britain
by Amazon

86291853R00174